Why Mit   ow
was beyond him.

"There's one thing I know for sure," he said. "This conversation, watching you—you're helping me find the answers I need."

"Really?"

A pleased expression lit up her face, transforming Fran into the most beautiful, desirable woman he'd ever seen. Hardly aware of his actions, he slid off the stool. "There's more," he said, rounding the counter and advancing toward her. "Something I just now realized."

"What's that?" Fran stayed where she was, her hands behind her, gripping the edge of the sink.

"You inspire me."

She swallowed. "That's quite a compliment."

Inches away from her, he stopped. "Trouble is, right now it's hard to concentrate." Mitch cupped her face and looked deeply into her eyes. "All I think about is kissing you."

She wrapped her arms around his neck. "Then do it."

Dear Reader,

This third and final story set in the fictitious seaside town of Cranberry, Oregon, is Fran's book. Stubby and Stumpy are back, as well as some of your favorite characters from *The Man She'll Marry* (June '06) and *It Happened One Wedding* (April '07).

Mitch Matthews is a motivation expert with one small problem: he can't motivate himself to write his book, and he's under a deadline. Hoping a change of scenery will help, he checks in to the Oceanside, where he has stayed many times, for an extended visit. This time without a beautiful woman to keep him company. Fran has always been a little in love with the handsome, dynamic Mitch. But she never imagined that… Well, you'll have to read the book to find out what happens.

I thoroughly enjoyed writing this series and welcome your continued e-mails and letters. Visit my Web site at www.annroth.net, e-mail me at ann@annroth.net, or write to me at Ann Roth, P.O. Box 25003, Seattle, WA 98165-1903.

Happy reading!

Ann Roth

MITCH TAKES A WIFE

Ann Roth

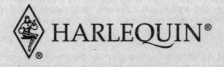

HARLEQUIN®

TORONTO • NEW YORK • LONDON
AMSTERDAM • PARIS • SYDNEY • HAMBURG
STOCKHOLM • ATHENS • TOKYO • MILAN • MADRID
PRAGUE • WARSAW • BUDAPEST • AUCKLAND

ISBN-13: 978-0-373-75178-5
ISBN-10:   0-373-75178-8

MITCH TAKES A WIFE

This edition published by arrangement with Harlequin Books S.A.

® and TM are trademarks of the publisher. Trademarks indicated with ® are registered in the United States Patent and Trademark Office, the Canadian Trade Marks Office and in other countries.

www.eHarlequin.com

Printed in U.S.A.

ABOUT THE AUTHOR

Ann Roth has always been a voracious reader of everything from classics to mysteries to romance. Of all the books she's read, love stories have affected her the most, and stayed with her the longest. A firm believer in the power of love, Ann enjoys creating emotional stories that illustrate how love can triumph over seemingly insurmountable odds.

Ann lives in the greater Seattle area with her husband and a really irritating cat who expects her breakfast no later than 6:00 a.m., seven days a week.

She would love to hear from readers. You can write her c/o P.O. Box 25003, Seattle, WA 98165-1903 or e-mail her at ann@annroth.net.

Books by Ann Roth

HARLEQUIN AMERICAN ROMANCE

To Mom and Dad. Your love and support
mean the world to me. You're in this book.
I hope you find yourselves!

Chapter One

Even with the kitchen faucet running and an Indigo Girls CD turned up high, Fran Bishop heard the crunch of gravel as a car rolled up the driveway on the other side of the building. Partly because she'd taken advantage of the unseasonably warm late-September afternoon and had opened the windows and sliding-glass door, but she'd also been waiting for the sound—for Mitch Matthews.

He'd booked the best room in the Oceanside Bed-and-Breakfast, the third-floor Orca Suite, for five weeks. The same room he always chose. This time though, he was coming to stay at the tail end of tourist season and was alone. He'd never stayed here more than a week, and never without a beautiful woman to keep him company.

Most tourists were long gone. Starting tomorrow, until the annual Cranberry Festival the third week of October, Mitch was Fran's only guest.

The car door slammed. With more anticipation than she had any right to feel, Fran shut off the music, dried her hands on her apron and then hung it on the hook behind the basement door. She barely had time to straighten her braid and smooth her yellow blouse over her dark green cords before Mitch's footsteps thudded across the planking of the ocean-view deck. The knocker hit the door twice—Mitch never used the buzzer—with crisp, staccato raps.

Already smiling and stifling the urge to hurry, she moved through the dining and great rooms and across to the entry. She opened the door. "Welcome, Mitch."

"Hello, Fran."

His grin was as irresistible as ever. He moved past her, bringing the tang of the sea air with him. At five feet ten in her socks, she wasn't small, yet Mitch stood a good five inches taller. A big, powerful man and handsome to boot.

While she silently admired his broad shoulders and strong jaw, he set down two large bags and a laptop computer case.

"It's good to see you," he said, his gray eyes mirroring the words.

She felt her cheeks warm with pleasure. "And you. When you didn't book a room over the summer, I thought that, after five years, you were tired of Cranberry or the Oceanside."

"I'll never get tired of you, the Oceanside or the Oregon coast," he said. "Thank God for this oasis."

"Oasis, huh? Can I quote you on my Web site?"

"Sure." He sniffed the air. "Something smells good, but around here, it usually does."

Mitch's ability to see the best in a person and offer genuine compliments, combined with his looks and skills as a motivational speaker and writer, were what drew people to him. He certainly made Fran feel good. Her smile widened.

"What you smell is my work in progress," she said. "I'm working on a recipe for the Cranberry cook-off, the event that kicks off the Cranberry Festival."

Mitch nodded. "I read about that on the 'net. Sounds interesting."

"It always is. Especially this year. The Food Network will be here, filming the contest."

The publicity would bring attention to Cranberry, where the locals depended heavily on tourism to survive. Fran hoped to be this year's grand-champion ribbon, which meant winning in her category and then beating out other category winners in a final round. The overall winner earned ten thousand dollars, among other prizes. Running the bed-and-breakfast was expensive and, with no income November through January, she barely kept afloat. And, after recently putting on a new roof… The cost had been staggering. Her savings were nearly gone, and prize money would go a long way toward replenishing them.

But better than the money was the chance of interesting the Food Network in a cookbook of her own, an otherwise near-to-impossible feat for an unknown cook.

"I really want to win the grand championship," she said.

"With your culinary skills?" Mitch smacked his lips. "You're a shoo-in."

She laughed. "Wait until you taste my entry before you say that. But if you do, you can't tell a soul what it is. I don't want any of my friends stealing my idea."

"Your secret will be safe with me. I noticed another

car in the driveway. I didn't realize anyone else would be here this late in the season."

"Only one couple, the Hortons from Sacramento. They're upstairs now, but they'll be down for the wine-and-cheese social." The get-together was a daily, late-afternoon ritual Fran offered her guests. "They've read your books and attended one of your seminars at the hospital where they work. They're eager to meet you."

"Just what I wanted to do, make small talk with strangers," Mitch muttered with a pained expression.

Since he'd always been an outgoing, friendly man, this surprised Fran. "I shouldn't have mentioned your name to them," she said. "But you always like meeting new people and I thought… Never mind. They're leaving tomorrow after breakfast. Then you're my only guest until the Cranberry Festival." For that popular week all seven rooms at the Oceanside were reserved.

"That's what I hoped for—solitude. My editor expects a book the first of November and I'll be finishing the thing while I'm here."

"The book I read about, on finding your bliss?" As a reasonably contented but sometimes lonely woman, Fran looked forward to gaining insight into living a happier life. "Sounds like an interesting topic."

His three previous books were filled with a wisdom and common sense she admired. She kept autographed copies of each on the bookcase that divided the dining room from the great room, for guests looking for something to read during their stay.

"It's interesting, all right."

Though he was smiling again, Fran couldn't help but sense a great heaviness, as though he carried the weight of who knew what on his back. She wanted to reach out, brush the hair off his forehead and somehow ease his burdens, but she had no business touching him.

"How are you?" she asked, studying him.

"Couldn't be better."

An automatic response. He'd always been upbeat, at least during his stays here. After all, he made his living motivating others. What in the world had caused this darker, sadder mood?

Since she wasn't about to ask—Mitch was her guest and, as such, deserved his privacy—she'd never know. What she *could* do was take care of him the best way she knew how. With delicious, hearty breakfasts, welcoming, comfortable surroundings and the peace and quiet he wanted.

"I'll just explain to the Hortons that you need to finish the book. They're nice people. They'll understand."

"Please don't do that. I don't want anyone to know it isn't done." His gaze sought hers. "Can I trust you to keep my situation private?"

The pleading look was another she'd never seen. She didn't understand his need for secrecy, but she wasn't a woman to betray a confidence. Besides, with Mitch staring intently and soberly into her eyes, she'd have promised him anything. "Of course."

He let out a relieved breath. "Good."

"I'll tell them you're tired."

"Which is the truth. No, if they're expecting to meet me, I won't disappoint them. But starting tomorrow, you can forget about the wine and cheese. Don't plan on seeing much of me."

Normally Fran set out cheese and crackers, opened

the wine and then retreated to her two-bedroom, basement apartment. But with Mitch as the only guest, she'd been looking forward to joining him for the hour, just the two of them talking and getting to know each other better.

Disappointed, she nodded. "All right, no afternoon snacks. What about breakfast?" Sumptuous breakfasts were included in the price. "You still want that, don't you? A good meal to start the day will give you the energy you need to work."

"That's one of the things I like about you, Fran. You take good care of me." His mouth twitched and the sorrow eased from the planes of his face, turning him into the Mitch she knew. "I wouldn't miss your breakfasts for anything. Now, I'd like to take my things upstairs and wash up before the socializing starts."

She nodded. "Would you like help with your bags?"

"No, thanks."

Slinging the strap of the laptop case over his shoulder, then hefting one suitcase in each hand, he headed for the wide, spiral staircase. Moments later, he disappeared.

His demeanor left Fran both worried and determined. She may not ever learn what had taken the light from Mitch's eyes, but she would do everything possible to give him what he needed. Peace, tranquility and privacy.

MITCH SET HIS BAGS on the thick carpet in the luxurious bedroom of the Orca Suite. He moved to the sitting room and laid his laptop on the desk that faced the ocean—his work space for the next five weeks. The top-floor suite, the best in the place, took up the entire third floor. Private and pleasant, with both a shower and soaker tub for two in the bathroom, the suite made for great romance. He'd never been here in the fall, and never without one woman or another. With a large-view window and balcony facing east and overlooking the ocean, the wood fireplace and cheery décor, the suite felt warm and inviting, even without a lover in tow. Exactly what he needed. He opened the sliding-glass door and strode onto the small balcony.

A chilly, salt-scented breeze ruffled the drapes and his hair, signaling a cool night ahead. The sun was about to set and the tide was on its way in. Waves rushed and foamed over the beach and the color slowly leached out of what had been a deep, blue sky. Gulls and pelicans circled over the water in search of fish.

Mitch inhaled the air and felt better than he had in a long while. The town, the sea, this house were salves to his sorry soul. So were Fran's nurturing ways. But then, her natural warmth always had drawn him.

He was looking forward to five weeks away from the energy-sucking people in his life, each with needs and demands. Especially his editor, agent and publicist. After pushing back his deadline twice, he had no choice but to complete the book he owed them. Everyone thought he'd finished the thing and was here to revise and polish it. Truth was, it has only half written, and badly. One hundred and fifty pages of pure garbage.

The motivation guru couldn't motivate himself. Now, there was something to write a book about. He snorted.

What in hell had possessed him to think he could write a book about finding your bliss? Did bliss even exist? Hell, if he knew. He scrubbed a hand over his face. Since his father had died eight months ago, he no longer knew much of anything. What he needed was time to think and sort out his life. Unfortunately, he didn't have that luxury.

Two pelicans dive-bombed into the sea, an enjoyable sight Mitch barely registered. Though he and his father never had been close, his death had ripped Mitch apart and affected him in ways he'd never imagined.

His creativity had all but dried up.

The instant the thought formed, his gut clenched in fear. *Only the weak let emotions get in the way of work,* his father always said. Mitch was not weak. He would drive out the demons and forge ahead. Setting his jaw, he willed away the anxiety.

Triumphant—for now—he relaxed. The one saving grace was, not a soul knew about his little problem, and no one ever would.

Like it or not, he was his father's son. They both were workaholics and given to stifle their feelings and move from woman to woman. True, there'd been a time when his dad had been faithful to his mother. But, since her death when Mitch was ten, the old man had been with countless women. Nothing serious and never for long.

Mitch had followed in those footsteps. He'd been fine that way, too. Until his father had set him thinking.

"Don't end up like me, son," he'd counseled in the weeks before he died. "Find a good woman, settle down and raise some kids. Put your career second, and you just might end up happy."

Surprising advice, and ironic, considering that Mitch was supposed to be the expert on happiness. He snickered.

So far no one realized he was a fraud. The motivational business he'd built from scratch was flourishing. His books made all the lists and businesses around the country wanted him for conferences and retreats. Now his agent and publicist were pressuring him to expand into the worldwide market. The time was right and Mitch knew without a doubt that he would triple his business and vastly increase his already impressive wealth.

Ten months ago, he'd have grabbed on to the idea and run with it. Now, after those last few weeks when he and his father had grown close, his father's advice ran continuously through his head. Mitch no longer knew what he wanted, except to regain his zest for life.

Would getting married help? If he ever met the right woman. For a while, with Mona, he'd thought he had.

They dated four months. An ad executive, she worked as hard as he did and seemed satisfied with their relationship. Mitch never knew for sure. He'd grown up in a home where you stifled your passions and uncertainty and, apparently, Mona had, too. Though they never talked about anything deep, never shared their hopes and fears, they got along well enough that, for a short while, he'd seriously considered marrying her.

But things hadn't worked out and they'd gone their separate ways. The sad part of that was, Mitch wasn't all that sorry. And, although he wanted to follow his father's advice, he wasn't sure he was built for marriage.

The wind gusted, this time hard enough to whip the cold air straight through him. He headed inside, pulling the sliding door closed behind him. Time for the dreaded wine-and-cheese social. He'd stick around for half an hour, then drive someplace for take-out, bring it home and eat up here. Turn in early and wake up refreshed and ready to work.

Come tomorrow, he'd hole up here and write the book—no excuses.

NORMALLY FRAN set out the wine and cheese and left visitors to it. But over the past few days, Tom and Jan Horton, her friendly, fortysomething guests, had invited her to stay. She'd enjoyed getting to know them. On this, their last night in town, she again joined them.

Bundled in sweaters, they carried their glasses and the cheese platter to the deck, where they could watch and smell the sea and hear the cries of the gulls over the crash of the waves.

"What do you think of Cranberry?" Fran asked. This was their first visit here.

"The town is charming and the beach, incredible," Jan said. "And this place is awesome. You made us feel warm and welcome, like family." She let out a wistful sigh. "I hate to leave."

"It's been a great four days," Tom agreed. "When the alarm rings Monday morning and we have go to work, it'll be painful."

Repeat customers made up a large part of Fran's clientele and she hoped they'd return. "Will you be back next year?"

"In early August," Jan said. "We thought we'd reserve a room now."

"I book up early, so that's wise." Fran got up to retrieve the reservation book from a drawer in the kitchen, which doubled as her office. She also grabbed a second bottle of wine, since they'd finished the first.

The couple supplied dates and their credit card, and Fran penciled them in. She set the book on a redwood patio table, beside the newly opened bottle. Then, with their redwood chairs lined up against the wood siding of the house, they sipped their wine, munched on cheese and crackers and watched the sky darken. For the most part, they were silent, but from time to time they exchanged comments.

"Tell us about Mitch Matthews," Jan said.

"Besides what you already know?" Fran searched her mind for a way to supply information without revealing too much. "This is his sixth year to stay here."

"Really? Wow, that's some endorsement." Jan shook her head. "Last year he did two seminars at our hospital, one for admin people and one for the medical staff. We all benefited. Thanks to Mitch, I think I'm better at my job."

Tom nodded. "I've been a physical therapist for twenty years. I was burned out until Mitch helped me see my work in a different light. I'm happy again and using some of his motivational techniques with my patients."

"I'm sure he'll enjoy hearing about that," Fran said.

"If he ever shows up." In the dusk Tom squinted at his watch. "Our dinner reservations are for seven-thirty. We'll be leaving soon."

Fran was beginning to wonder whether Mitch would join them. "He said he'd be here."

Though he could've changed his mind. She glanced inside, through the sliding-glass door that opened into the dining room. She'd shut it against the rapidly cooling night air. There he was, striding toward her. How did such a big man move so gracefully?

She'd left on lights inside, making it easy to study him through the glass. He'd changed into a navy turtle-neck sweater—a wise move, given the chill. The wool lovingly draped his shoulders and solid torso. Such a well-proportioned, gorgeous man. No wonder he had his pick of beautiful women.

She set down her glass, then gestured toward the house. "There he is, now."

As Jan and Tom craned their necks, Mitch stopped at the pearl-colored serving counter that divided the dining room from the kitchen. There, Fran had left him a clean wineglass. He grabbed it, then headed around the dining-room table to the slider.

The sliding door opened, and both Tom and Jan stood to greet him.

After the introductions, Mitch sat down beside Fran, so that she was between him and the Hortons. He filled his glass, then stared at the sky and sea rather than the Hortons. Undeterred, they chattered away, their Mitch-directed comments forcing his attention.

He responded with his characteristic appeal, appearing to be interested in the couple and their work. He didn't mention his upcoming book, and when they did, glossed over a reply before skillfully deflecting their questions onto themselves, so that they did most of the talking, which made them like him all the more. If Fran hadn't known him as well as she did, she'd never have guessed he was pretending.

Again she wondered what had happened. A broken

heart? But Mitch didn't fall in love. At least, he hadn't over the five years she'd known him.

Tom's watch beeped. With genuine regret he glanced at Jan. "Time to go." To Mitch he explained, "Dinner reservations in town."

Everyone stood. Mitch shook hands with Tom, then with Jan, who seemed as dazzled as if she were standing before a movie star. Mitch was that good-looking and that charismatic. When they mentioned that they looked forward to sharing breakfast with Mitch before they left, he replied that he did, too.

Fran and Mitch remained standing, Fran in the threshold of the gaping slider. When Jan and Tom finally walked out the front door and shut it behind them, Mitch exhaled a loud breath.

"I thought they'd never leave."

Fran turned toward him. "You used to enjoy meeting people. You said you liked making new friends."

"Did I?" Light from the house touched his cheeks and forehead but left his eyes in shadow. "I'm sick to death of small talk," he said, and she assumed that meant talking to her, too.

That stung, but Fran understood. He wanted to be alone. "You've done your duty for today," she said, forcing a smile. "If you want dinner you should probably go now, while the restaurants are open."

"I don't feel like going out. I suppose you have plans tonight? A date with some lucky guy?"

Oh, she had a date, all right. With leftover pot roast, a few mindless TV shows and a magazine or two. A pathetic way to spend a Saturday night, but she was used to it. She shook her head. But, having skipped the cheese and crackers, she was famished. And Mitch had practically come out and told her to leave him alone. "It's a beautiful evening. I'll leave you to enjoy it." She started through the threshold.

"Wait." He clasped her shoulder.

Even through her bulky cardigan she felt the warmth of his fingers and the solid weight of his hand. He'd never touched her before. Unsure what to make of this, she turned toward him…and thought she saw heat flicker in his eyes.

She was flattered, but only for a moment. Mitch Matthews was her guest and a friend. Nothing more. Still, her heart fluttered.

"Yes, Mitch?"

Dropping his hand and his gaze, he stepped back, as if he wished he hadn't touched her. She'd definitely imagined his interest. No more wine for her.

"We both need dinner, right? We may as well eat together. Why don't we order a pizza?"

Who knew, maybe he'd confide in her, tell her his troubles. Plenty of other people did. Fran wanted to help. She also wanted to spend more time with him. With him so busy and wanting time alone, this might be her only chance to do so. "Pizza sounds good," she said.

In the light spilling from the dining room she thought Mitch looked relieved. Yes, he definitely wanted her company.

Aware that she felt far too pleased about that, she piled the wine bottles and Tom and Jan's glasses onto the empty cheese platter. Mitch started to follow her into the house. She didn't want him inside the house with her, not now. She needed time to compose herself.

"You stay out here and enjoy the evening, while I order the pizza."

Setting the tray on the dining-room table, she firmly pulled the slider shut.

Chapter Two

While Fran was inside ordering pizza, Mitch sat in a deck chair, stared into the darkness and swore. He'd come here to be alone, had craved isolation so badly that he'd driven nine hours from Seattle to get here. So why had he invited Fran to eat with him? They'd never shared a meal before. In the past, he and whatever woman he was with had breakfasted with the other guests, while Fran stood ready to replenish platters and refill coffee mugs. He never saw her at night.

Even though she was a warm, attractive woman he'd never thought about kissing her until a few minutes ago. That was a lie. No red-blooded male could help wondering what she'd taste like. But never before had his thoughts progressed beyond mild interest.

Yet, for a moment there tonight, right before she went inside, he'd wanted badly to find out if she was as sweet as she looked, which was his nuttiest idea yet. Fran was everything he wasn't—warm and nurturing. He liked her. But he was her guest, period, with a book to write. He'd come here to avoid distractions, not create more.

She was a friend and only a friend. Tonight, he needed her company because… Because. Mitch didn't want to probe that question. He already had enough on his plate. The great thing about Fran was, she wouldn't pry into his life or ask anything of him. This one evening together was all he wanted, a relaxed few hours with enjoyable conversation and no pretense. Only, she'd do most of the talking. Mitch excelled at getting others to talk so he wouldn't have to.

She would tell him about herself, and, after they ate, he'd head upstairs and get a good night's rest, exactly as he'd planned. Come morning, after breakfast and more polite chitchat, he'd shut himself in the suite and work. No excuses, no delays, no mental blocks. *Got that, buddy?*

The kitchen and dining rooms went dark and the tiny white lights lining the deck railing blinked on. The slider opened. Fran slipped through with a fresh bottle of wine. Leaving the door open a crack she set the bottle on the table within his reach. She sat down, the table between them.

"The pizza should be here in thirty minutes," she said as she refilled his glass.

Her own had disappeared. "You're not drinking tonight?"

"Not anymore. I've had enough."

He suspected she'd had enough of more than wine. Taking care of people all the time had to be draining. "Bet you'll be glad when tourist season ends."

"I will. Don't get me wrong, I love what I do. But, after working seven days a week since May, I'm ready for a break."

"Would you rather I stay someplace else?" he asked, knowing she'd say no, but all the same feeling the need to ask.

Without a second's hesitation she shook her head. "You're no problem at all."

"That's a relief." He smiled. "Tell me, Fran, what do you do in the off-season? Travel?"

"Not this year. I spent my vacation money on a new roof."

"So how do you fill your days when there are no guests here?"

"Do you really want to know?"

Mitch did, and he nodded.

"Well, sometimes I take classes at the local community college. I get together with friends I'm too busy to see during tourist season. Catch up on my reading and my knitting. Occasionally I rent out the great room for parties or weddings. Which reminds me, I'm hosting a baby shower for Cinnamon Mahoney in a few weeks. You remember her."

He did. Cinnamon, who ran the employee-owned cranberry factory, was Fran's closest friend. He nodded. "A baby shower, huh? She hasn't been married that long."

"Almost two and a half years. She's due November fifteenth." Fran shot him an apologetic look. "I didn't know you wanted solitude. But since you're on the third floor, the noise shouldn't bother you."

"Probably not," Mitch said, making a mental note to buy earplugs.

"I'm also working on that cook-off entry. If I win—"

"Not *if*," Mitch corrected. "*When*. Think positive."

"Point taken, Mr. Motivational Guru. *When* I win the contest I'll talk to the Food Network people about a brunch cookbook I'd like to publish. Fine-tuning those recipes will take time. And I should update my Web site and brochure for next year."

She glanced at him, and he nodded that he wanted to hear more.

"What else? I'm volunteering at this year's Cranberry Festival. I won't be working at the festival itself, but there's plenty of advance work needed to make sure it runs smoothly. You wouldn't believe what that entails—meetings and phone calls and running around. Once the festival ends, any needed repairs to the house start. Nick Mahoney, Cinnamon's husband—remember him? He's my handyman—takes care of most of that." She waved her hand through the air in a dismissive gesture. "The list goes on and on."

She sounded like any smart, savvy businesswoman. Interesting, but Mitch wanted more personal stuff. "What about your nights? Dating anyone?"

He was good at reading people, and the question flustered her. Her discomfort piqued his curiosity all the more.

"Not in a while," she said, glancing at her lap.

"A beautiful woman like you? I don't believe it."

"I'm not beautiful."

The light from the stringer around the deck was bright enough that he saw the flush coloring her cheeks. "I think so. Any man who doesn't is blind."

"You're full of it, Mitch Matthews," Fran said, looking pleased, despite her words. After a beat of silence, she spoke again. "I do have exciting news. I'm about to become a godparent to Cinnamon and Nick's baby!"

Her smile and enthusiasm were genuine, yet, beneath that, he sensed a sadness. Why?

"They're having a girl—Callie. So I'll be reading up on babies."

"Wow." Mitch shook his head. "I don't know the first thing about kids, but I do know that, with your nurturing ways, you'll make a great godparent." A great mother, too. Warm and loving, the kind every kid should have. Mitch hadn't been so lucky. His own mother had been cool and reserved. "Why hasn't some great guy married you?"

"I was engaged once." A sad smile curled her lips. "But then—"

The buzzer rang before she finished. "There's the pizza." She jumped up.

Wondering what she'd been about to say and determined to find out later, Mitch stood, too. "I'll get this." He snagged her wrist. "You relax."

It was the second time he'd touched her tonight. He couldn't seem to stop himself. Her wrist was small-boned and easy to circle. He caught the scent of vanilla and, under that, of woman. His body responded with amazing speed, the urge to kiss her almost overpowering.

"Are you sure?" Fran asked.

He had no idea what she meant. "Am I sure?" he repeated, placing her palm on his chest, where she could feel his heartbeat.

She tipped up her chin and searched his eyes. "Mitch, I—"

The buzzer sounded again, this time for several seconds. A rude, but timely interruption. What had come over him tonight?

He released her. "*I* invited *you* to share this pizza," he said. And he needed to get away from her to clear his head. "Stay put."

"Okay. Thanks." She sank back onto her chair.

As Mitch strode into the house and headed for the front door, he pulled in a breath. The whole place smelled of vanilla. Of Fran.

His blood stirred and he knew he was in trouble.

WHILE MITCH PAID for the pizza, Fran stared past the lights along the railing, barely registering the pitch blackness or the soft rush of the ocean.

He'd almost kissed her. She'd almost let him.

She marveled at her perfectly calm hand, which he'd placed directly over his pounding heart. That and the questions he'd asked tonight went beyond causal. He was a good listener, and she'd found herself wanting to tell him the most personal and painful things. About her miscarriage and subsequent broken engagement eight years ago. And how her aunt Frannie had taken her in, no questions asked, while Fran nursed her broken heart and mourned her empty womb. She'd only been ten weeks along but she'd loved the baby growing inside her.

The pain from Leif's walking away was long gone, and she'd thought she'd moved past losing the baby. But lately… While she was thrilled for Cinnamon and Nick, their pregnancy had stirred up the old ache for the child she would've had. She'd never admitted this to Cinnamon. Why dampen her best friend's happiness over something that had happened years ago? Besides, talking about it only made it worse.

Yet, if not for the arrival of the pizza man Fran would have shared everything with Mitch. He truly seemed interested. As a friend. But also as a man.

And that put her right back at their almost-kiss.

The current between them tonight was new. Where had it come from? Certainly, she'd always harbored a secret crush on Mitch. He was a sexy man. And, yes, now and then he'd looked at her with extra warmth. But nothing like tonight.

Was she to be this year's vacation fling? The instant the question entered her head she brushed it away. Of course not. She wasn't interested in a fling. Neither was Mitch. He wanted solitude. Still, whatever had changed and sobered him also had subtly shifted their relationship. Fran needed to know why.

Mitch returned with the pizza. He opened the box, releasing the smells of cheese, sausage and olives. Her mouth watering, Fran handed him a plate, then helped herself. Mitch followed suit, and, for a while, neither of them spoke. From lowered lashes, she glanced at him. Chewing methodically while he fixed his gaze on the darkness, he seemed as tense and unsettled as she was.

She nearly lost her nerve, but curiosity won out.

"Mitch?" she said, as he reached for a second slice of pizza. "If you don't mind my saying so, you seem... different. Unhappy."

"Do I?"

His mouth twisted, either in a grimace or a semblance of a smile—she didn't know which. She nodded.

"Should've known I couldn't fool you." His bleak gaze connected with hers before he reached for a napkin. "Earlier this year, I lost my father."

Now Fran understood the heavy sorrow that clung to him like the morning mist. Maybe the physical awareness between them stemmed from his loss and the need to connect.

"That's rough," she murmured with heartfelt sympathy. "Years ago, I lost both my parents and later Aunt Frannie—my aunt, who left me the Oceanside. I still miss them." *And sometimes the child I would have had.* She thought about telling him, but this wasn't about her. "I'm sorry, Mitch."

"Thanks. We weren't close until the end, but I miss him like hell."

She wanted to hold out her arms and offer comfort, but given the heightened awareness between them, that wasn't a good idea. So she gave him the next best thing—an accepting silence.

A few seconds ticked by before he nodded at her. "That's another thing I like about you, Fran. I can be myself around you and know you won't nose into my private life."

She'd heard this before. "Everyone says I'm a lot like my aunt." Frannie had never married, but had led a full life catering to others.

Mitch returned to his meal, making quick work of three more slices of pizza. The man ate like a football player after a game. Fran fiddled with a crust, all that remained of her second slice.

Her aunt may have been satisfied living her days alone. Not Fran. It had taken eight years, but at long last, she was ready to fall in love and settle down. She wanted what Cinnamon and Nick had—a happy home, marriage and children.

Unfortunately, she was thirty-two, without a marriage-minded man in sight. Want to or not, she probably would end up a childless old spinster, the same as her aunt. No longer hungry, she dropped her crumpled napkin on her plate.

"So you were engaged once," Mitch said, returning to their before-pizza conversation. "What happened?"

Now that he'd asked, she found that she couldn't talk about the miscarriage. "Things changed and he walked out."

"He was a damned fool."

"It was a long time ago. I'm over it now." She shrugged. "Pizza was exactly what I needed. Thank you, Mitch."

"My pleasure," he said, glancing at her mouth.

Pleasure. The word resounded through her, evoking hot and interesting images. Mitch had been with so many women. He probably knew exactly how to give pleasure.

Fran hadn't been with a man in longer than she cared to think about. Heat licked her insides. Feeling foolish, she stacked their plates. "It's late, and you know I get up at five-thirty to make breakfast. I'm sure you're tired, too. We both should go to bed."

The instant she uttered the words, she flushed. She jerked up her gaze to find Mitch studying her with open interest.

"Not without dessert," he said in a dark, smoothly suggestive voice.

Did he mean food or something else? Suddenly nervous, Fran fiddled with her braid. "I don't have anything to offer you."

Except herself. *Stop it!*

"Sure you do," he said. "Some of that cook-off entry I smelled earlier."

Disappointed and at the same time relieved, she let out a breath. "I guess the smell was a dead giveaway. They're for the dessert category. Cranberry bars, but I haven't nearly perfected the recipe yet."

"I still want a taste."

"Okay, but don't say I didn't warn you. And remember, this is top secret. I don't want any of my competition to know a thing, not even which category I've entered."

"I swear to keep my yap shut," he said, sounding like a B-grade actor in a cops-and-robbers film.

She grinned. "That's good enough for me. It's cold out here. Let's go inside."

As MITCH STUFFED half a cranberry bar into his mouth, Fran chewed a tiny bite, cocked her head toward the ceiling and frowned. "It needs something."

With his own mouth full, he didn't reply. They were sitting on stools on opposite sides of the counter that separated the kitchen from the dining room.

A crumb had settled in the corner of her mouth. He thought about brushing it away but decided against it. He wasn't about to touch her again.

At a gesture from him, she licked off the offending crumb. The innocent flick of her tongue really messed with him, fueling his imagination. Tearing his attention away from her lips, he swallowed his mouthful. "It's not bad. Much better than anything I could make."

"But you don't cook. Come on, Mitch, tell the truth."

"All right, it could be better. Just don't ask me how to fix it."

"I appreciate your honesty. Making it better is my problem." She sighed. "Tomorrow, it's back to the drawing board."

She carried their plates to the sink. She was tall and long-legged, dressed in the bright colors she favored. A while ago she'd taken off her sweater and her loose yellow blouse amplified her breasts. Mitch was a breast man, and hers were big and soft-looking.

Her thick brown braid swished across her back. He imagined her hair loose and streaming down her bare skin. Then spread across the sheets as she lay under him...

Yeah, right. He hadn't come to the Oceanside for that. He was here to work. Mitch cleared his throat. "How exactly does one create a decent recipe?"

"Oh, it's very scientific." Smiling, she returned to her stool. "Add this, cut that, bake and taste."

He liked the sound of that. "I volunteer here and now to be your official, scientific taste tester."

The laugh that bubbled from her throat brought out his own grin.

"But you don't have time."

"Throw away the chance to help you win the contest? You need me," he teased. "And I'll be satisfying my sweet tooth at the same time. I definitely have time for that."

"All right, you've got yourself a deal."

"Excellent." He did what he always did when he sealed a deal—shook her hand.

Her fingers were warm and so were her eyes. They were hazel, which he hadn't realized until now.

Mitch did not release her hand. Awareness bloomed in her expression. His blood stirred as it hadn't in a long time, and he forgot that he shouldn't want her.

He turned her hand over, exposing the inside of her wrist. His thumb ran tiny circles over the sensitive place above her palm. He felt her pulse bump and noted her enlarged pupils. Her lips parted, and a certain part of him woke up.

It'd be so easy to lean across the counter and kiss her....

But this was *Fran*. He released her hand. At the same time, as if she'd read his mind and agreed with him, she pulled out of his grasp and averted her eyes.

"Better clean up," she said, sliding off the stool.

Brisk and cool, she brushed crumbs from the counter into her palm.

She was as rattled as he was.

"Hey."

"What?" She moved to the sink and dusted off her hands.

"Fran. Look at me."

At last, she stilled and faced him.

"I don't know what just happened, but I was out of line. Your friendship is important to me and I'd hate to think I screwed that up. Are we okay?"

After a moment, she nodded. "We're fine, Mitch."

The uncertainty in her eyes belied the words and worried him. He hoped that, after a good night's sleep, everything would return to normal.

Chapter Three

Sunday morning, while Mitch and the Hortons talked over breakfast at the dining-room table, Fran stayed busy in the kitchen. Keeping a watchful eye on her guests, she refilled juice glasses with cranberry or orange juice—because of the local cranberry factory, the town insisted that all businesses offering breakfast serve cranberry juice. She also topped off coffee mugs when needed and replenished the French toast, scrambled eggs and sausage platters. She readied Melmac plates for Stubby and Stumpy, the seagulls she'd fed daily since each had first landed on her deck railing several years ago. They expected to dine on exactly what the guests ate, freshly cooked and piping hot.

The wall of windows and floor-to-ceiling glass sliding door allowed everyone full view of the entertaining gulls, Stubby minus the webbing on one foot and Stumpy with a bum leg permanently folded under him. Both waited on the railing with open beaks aimed toward the three humans in the dining room. They knew what was coming and seemed to enjoy the attention from whomever sat at the table.

This morning, Jan and Tom ate with their backs to Fran. Mitch was across from them, facing her.

He was dressed in jeans and a white cotton shirt with the cuffs rolled up, and he looked ruggedly handsome. Every time she glanced up, he was watching her. It was unnerving. She wished she could read his mind and wondered whether, despite his apology, he still was as bothered about last night as she was.

In the light of day, she realized that the wine she'd drunk had opened doors inside of her that were better left closed. If, for a few hours, they'd thought about kissing each other, at least Mitch had had the wisdom to pull back. Thank goodness, or how would she have faced him this morning?

"Look at the gulls, opening and closing their beaks and hopping along the railing," Jan said. "They look hungry and impatient. But then, they have every morning since we've been here."

"I'll bet the same thing happens even without us guests, every day all year 'round." Mitch glanced at Fran, his eyes clear and steady, and maybe a tad worried. "Am I right?"

He definitely was concerned, which meant he cared about their friendship, and that was a relief. "Every single morning." Plates in hand, she rounded the counter and the dining-room table, brushing past Mitch. "If someone will open the slider, I'll put an end to their misery."

"Great," Jan said. "I'll take a few more photos." A picture fanatic, she'd taken dozens over the past four mornings. She stood, moved to the window and readied her camera.

Mitch opened the slider. As Fran slipped through she caught a whiff of his clean, masculine scent. He hadn't shaved, and the stubble on his chin and cheeks added an adventurous, slightly wild air to him. So very sexy. Having learned her lesson last night, she avoided eye contact.

The cloudy, cool morning suited her mood. She could feel Mitch's gaze on her. Self-conscious, her heart lifting more than it had any business doing, she set the plates on the deck floor, moved out of his range of vision and waited for the gulls to hop down.

It was impossible to fool herself—even without wine she was hugely attracted to Mitch Matthews. Regardless, she wouldn't repeat last night's mistake. He would never know. From now on, it was breakfast with a smile, and if Mitch wanted conversation, small talk. Nothing more, period.

Satisfied with her plan, she watched Stubby and Stumpy claim their meals before she headed inside again.

For several minutes, everyone watched the gulls devour their food, and Jan snapped pictures. As breakfast wound down, the Hortons occupied Mitch's attention with comments and occasional questions. He treated them with the same warmth and interest he had last night. He could've had a career in acting.

"Will you be signing your new book in Sacramento?" Jan asked.

"That's something my publicist would know," Mitch said. "The information will be posted on my Web site around the time of publication, so check there."

While he was focused on Jan, Fran studied him. Though he appeared to be full of energy, she noted the weariness under that engaged expression. She hoped that nothing in the suite itself had disturbed his rest. Could it be that, after what had happened last night, he'd slept as badly as she had? Or possibly, he'd stayed up late, working?

While she mulled over the possible reasons for his sleepless night, he glanced up and caught her staring. His mouth quirked and one eyebrow arched a fraction—charming, as always.

Her gaze darted to his juice glass and she raised the cranberry pitcher from the counter. "You're low on juice, Mitch. How about a refill?"

"I'm good, thanks."

"Anyone else?" Fran asked.

"None for me," Tom said. "We're leaving soon. Before we go, could we get pictures with you, Mitch?"

"Why not?"

"Terrific." Jan handed her camera to Fran. "Would you do the honors?"

The gulls had finished and departed. Fran and her guests headed onto the deck, stepping over the empty plates. They stood with the ocean at their backs, Jan and Tom on either side of Mitch. He towered over both, smiling while the wind whipped his hair rakishly over his forehead.

Fran took three photos before the Hortons were satisfied. She returned their camera. They promised to e-mail the picture to her and to Mitch.

Twenty minutes later, they were gone. Time to clean up the kitchen and get on with the day. Fran expected Mitch to head upstairs and get to work but, instead, he hung around, clearing dishes and making himself useful.

"You're a guest here," she said. "You don't need to do this."

"I want to."

She wasn't about to refuse the help. For several minutes, they tidied the kitchen in silence.

When the table was cleared and the place mats wiped clean of crumbs, Mitch swiped his palms on his jeans. "That's that. What's on your agenda today?"

A harmless question. "Maid duty in the room where the Hortons stayed." During the busy summer months she hired a housekeeper, but, when things slowed down, she did the job herself to save money. "After that, errands."

"Then what?"

"Don't you have a book to finish?"

"Yeah." He shifted his weight, then shot her a guarded look. "I can sense your tension. Is there something you want to say?"

With his chin angled a fraction and the earnest look on his face, she couldn't very well lie. "To tell you the truth, I'm still a little embarrassed about last night."

"I was afraid of that. We both got caught in the moment." His gaze flitted briefly to her mouth. "I meant what I said last night. It won't happen again."

Believing him, Fran nodded.

"So we're friends?"

"Friends."

His relieved expression knocked out the last of her anxiety. Things really *were* back to normal.

"Before you go upstairs, my friend, let me give you a key to the front door." Opening the supplies drawer near the phone, Fran located a spare and dropped it into Mitch's hand.

"Now you don't have to worry about coming and going. I'll be out all afternoon and I'm having dinner at Cinnamon and Nick's." Her absence would give him the solitude he wanted. "Help yourself to anything in the kitchen," she added, "and, when you go out, take your key."

MITCH STARED at the blank computer screen with growing frustration. Despite the ocean view, despite the comfortable room and quiet surroundings, his mind refused to cooperate. With only five weeks to finish the rough draft of the book and shape it into reasonable condition, he ought to be pounding the keyboard. But the words would not come. He'd made things right with Fran, and had eaten an enjoyable and hearty breakfast. Yet his ideas had vanished, leaving him empty. He didn't know how to bring them back.

The fear that haunted him returned. Gritting his teeth he stood and paced to the window. Heavy clouds filled the sky and the ocean was gray and turbulent. He slipped onto the balcony. The damp, cold air bit his face like a bracing slap. A walk on the beach, that was what he needed. The fresh air and activity would help him think.

Only one problem—Fran hadn't gone out yet. She thought he was hard at work.

What a joke. *You'll never finish this book,* a voice in his head chided.

Mitch rubbed his hand over his face, the scratch of beard reminding him he hadn't shaved. Earlier, he hadn't felt the need, but the familiar routine might jar his brain. He would shave while he waited for Fran to drive away. Then walk the beach and banish this problem, once and for all.

As the electric razor buzzed over his chin he avoided his own eyes in the mirror. The stark grief he saw every time he glanced at his reflection disturbed him. If his father were still alive he'd have bullied the look right out of Mitch. But the man was dead, damn him. Mitch managed a wry smile. Thank God he knew how to hide his feelings from everyone else.

Although Fran had sensed the changes in him. She knew about his father but not the rest, and never would. She had no idea how badly he needed her warmth and acceptance. Mitch counted himself lucky that last night's lapse in judgment was behind them.

Through the bathroom window, which he'd cracked open for the fresh air, he heard tires crunch over the gravel. Peering over the frosted lower pane, he watched Fran's silver sedan back out of the garage. When she passed the weathered, Oceanside Bed-and-Breakfast sign and turned onto the road, he let out a breath. Feeling like a kid skipping school, he grabbed a sweatshirt, pocketed the door key and went downstairs.

In seconds, he was striding across the deck, the salty tang of the air filling his nostrils. Eager to reach the beach, he took the stairs that connected the deck with the ground two at a time. The ocean was a few yards away, and the soft swoosh-swoosh of the waves called to him with its siren song. Mitch trampled tall grasses and circled piles of aging driftwood. Then he was on the beach. The tide was going out and he moved close to the water, enjoying the soft suck of the wet sand against his sneakers.

A cold wind whipped around him, lifting the hair from his forehead, and he was glad for his sweatshirt. Setting off for no place in particular, he strode briskly along the shore, while pelicans and seagulls wheeled low over the sea.

Slightly winded, he rounded a curve around a bit of rocky shore. Ten feet ahead, a grizzle-haired man with a dirty duffel bag slung on his shoulder walked onto the beach. He saw Mitch, waved and moved toward him, his boots churning up sand.

Mitch had no choice but to wave back. He slowed to an easy walk.

"Nice day," the man said. Small and wiry, he looked to be in his sixties, with wild, curly hair and a few days' stubble on his face.

"Sure is."

Mitch eyed the rumpled shirt and patches on his worn pants and wool jacket and wondered if he was homeless, or a drunk. But his blue eyes were clear and bright.

"Haven't seen you around here."

"I don't live here."

"Tourist, huh? Where you staying?"

Mitch gestured toward the Oceanside, a good five hundred yards behind him. "The Oceanside."

"Fran Bishop's place. Back in the day, I knew her aunt Frannie. We went to school together. The Bishop women are good people. Name's Foster Gravis."

"Mitch Matthews."

They shook hands, Foster's grip callused and surprisingly strong. Mitch made a mental note to ask Fran about him.

"I'm lookin' for driftwood, if you care to help."

Why not? Better than brooding about his miserable life. Maybe the man needed firewood. "Sure," Mitch said.

The stuff littered the beach. Mitch picked up several sodden, sea-worn pieces. Eventually they would dry out. "You want these in the bag?"

Foster eyed the wood, then shook his head. "Those are too green and too boring. What I want has to have some character and be yea big," he said, gesturing with his hands. "I'm looking for something more weathered." He squinted at the sand, walked forward a few feet down and picked up a knotty, arm-sized, silvered chunk of wood. "Now this is bigger than what I need, but the lines are good. And I can cut it into smaller pieces. Here." He pointed. "And here."

"You're not looking for firewood."

"Not hardly." Foster chuckled. "I'm an artist. I carve sea creatures and birds and mount 'em on the driftwood."

Fascinating, and something Mitch never would've guessed. He spied a large, whorled piece of wood and hefted it. "Is this what you want?"

"Exactly. Put 'er in."

In no time, wood bulged from Foster's bag.

"Never filled it this fast," Foster said. "You have a good eye. You an artist, too?"

Mitch shook his head. "I'm an author and motivational speaker."

"Huh." Cocking his head, the old man eyeballed him. "Any good at it?"

Where was this leading? Mitch tensed. "Most of the time."

"That's how it is with me and the wood carving."

When he said nothing more, Mitch relaxed. "What do you do when you're not satisfied with what you're working on?"

"That depends. The wood talks to me. I can feel what's below the surface. If I like what I feel, I'll rework a piece umpteen times. But sometimes it's right to start fresh." Foster grasped the duffel handles. "This ought to keep me stocked for a while." Grunting with effort, he boosted it onto his shoulder.

The little man couldn't possibly handle all that weight. "Why don't you let me carry that?" Mitch offered.

"If you don't mind. Won't take but a minute. I live up there, right off the beach."

The thing weighed a ton. Ten minutes later, sweating, Mitch laid his load on the peeling, covered wood porch of Foster's bungalow. He glanced around as he wiped his brow.

Life-sized, meticulously detailed carvings of seals, otters, pelicans and gulls lined the yard and porch. "Did you carve all these?"

"Sure did. I'm in to the smaller stuff now, though."

Mitch wandered from carving to carving. In the yard he studied an otter, so beautifully made that his fur looked soft and real.

"These are fantastic. I'd like to buy one." Foster looked as if he could use the money, and Mitch genuinely liked his work.

"They aren't for sale. But thanks." He glanced at Mitch's hands. "If you wanted, I could teach you to carve."

An intriguing idea, but Mitch was here to write. Period. "No, thanks." He glanced at his watch, surprised to see that he'd been gone over an hour. "I'd best get back."

"See you around," Foster said. "Tell Fran hello."

Mitch headed back, wind-whipped and cold, his head in a far better place. He had no idea why, but Foster Gravis had brightened his day.

Chapter Four

By late Sunday afternoon Fran had finished her errands, just in time to head for Cinnamon and Nick's.

Humming, she turned onto a narrow, two-lane road that wound slowly upward toward a bluff that overlooked the ocean. The thick stand of madronas, evergreens and fir trees on both sides of the road made her feel as if she were the only person here, but that was an illusion.

Thanks in part to Cinnamon for leading an employee buyout of the once failing, now thriving cranberry factory, Cranberry was growing. Behind the trees, seasoned bungalows were intermixed with expensive new houses. Last year Nick and Cinnamon had built an ocean-view home up here.

Because of the busy tourist season and Cinnamon's job as general manager of the cranberry factory, Fran hadn't been here or seen her best friend in weeks. Eager to catch up with her, she pulled up the blacktop driveway. Seconds later, she was on her way to the kitchen door. The wind that buffeted her smelled of rain. She hurried forward, admiring the natural shake siding, which was beginning to silver nicely. Before she could knock at the door, Cinnamon flung it open.

"You're here!"

They shared a hug, made awkward by Cinnamon's advanced pregnancy. Pulling back, Fran studied her best friend, who wore a designer maternity dress, with wide eyes. "You've grown since I last saw you. You're huge."

"I know. I feel like a watermelon." Beaming, Cinnamon gestured Fran inside. "Nick thinks I'll deliver early."

"He does?" Fran followed her through the spacious, ultramodern kitchen, past the tasteful dining room and down a wide hallway decorated with photographs and paintings created by local artists. They reached the living room, which was as neat and elegantly put together as Cinnamon. The wall of windows and view deck faced the sea with a bird's-eye view similar to the B and B's. "What does Doc Bartlett say?"

"That I'm right on schedule. That means, eight more weeks to grow. I swear, if I get any bigger, I'll pop."

Nick, who'd come from upstairs where the bedrooms were, joined them. "Hello, Fran." He kissed her cheek before wrapping an arm around his wife's shoulder. "She looks beautiful, doesn't she?" A tender smile lit his face, and he laid a possessive hand over her belly.

"You need glasses," she said, looking pleased.

They shared a loving, intimate look Fran envied. She shook her head in wonder. "To think I introduced you two."

Cinnamon and Nick had met nearly three years ago, when Cinnamon had stayed at Fran's for a much-needed vacation. At the time, Nick had worked as a gifted handyman. Now a successful inventor, he still took care of odd jobs for Fran and a few other select people. She counted herself fortunate that he did. And was glad her best friend had married him.

"Why don't you two sit down and make yourselves comfortable?" Nick said. "I'll bring the drinks. You want wine, Fran?"

After last night, she'd sworn off the stuff, at least before dinner. She shook her head. "I'll have whatever Cinnamon drinks."

"Two sparkling grape juices, coming up."

As Nick headed for the kitchen, Fran and Cinnamon sat down on the fat, suede sofa that faced the view.

"How's Mitch?" Cinnamon asked. She'd met him a few times and knew he was staying at Fran's for five weeks. "Is he still as handsome and magnetic as ever?"

Fran debated what to say. That last night he'd almost kissed her—twice? That both times she'd wanted him to? But it was all behind them now, so why mention it?

"As charming as ever," she said. "On the surface, at least. Underneath, something's different."

Nick returned with drinks and a bowl of trail mix, which, for some reason, Cinnamon craved.

"I'm so excited about my baby shower," Cinnamon said, grabbing some. "Aren't you, Nick?"

He handed out the drinks with a deer-caught-in-the-headlights look. "Uh, not really. But it's either go or end up in the doghouse."

"That's my husband." Laughter bubbled from Cinnamon, who radiated happiness. "See how well trained he is?"

Not only that, but he adored her. The ache Fran had felt last night for her own baby was barely noticeable now. She felt too much love here for any other emotion. Even Mitch would smile watching Nick and Cinnamon together. Fran hoped the writing had gone well today and that he appreciated the peace and quiet.

Cinnamon's stomach gurgled. On the verge of sitting down, Nick changed his mind. "Hungry again?" He glanced at Fran. "She had a sandwich right before you showed up."

"I know, but my tummy wants food," Cinnamon said. "You'd think with my insides squished to nothing I'd have lost my appetite." She popped more trail mix into her mouth.

"You're eating for two," Nick teased. "I started the potatoes when I poured the drinks. Think I'll fire up the grill and start those steaks. Fran, will you help with the rest of the meal?"

"I'd love to."

Cinnamon shook her head. "She's been waiting on people all season and she's hosting our baby shower in a few weeks. This is her night to relax. Besides, it's not hard to make a salad and put the green beans into the steamer." She shot a scolding but loving look at her husband. "He's always babying me."

"I think it's sweet," Fran said, smiling.

"Thank you, Fran." Nick polished his nails on his shirt and left for the sheltered, backyard patio to start the grill.

Refusing Fran's help, Cinnamon struggled from the sofa. They returned to the kitchen.

"You were saying that Mitch is different," she said,

picking up their earlier conversation. "Exactly what does that mean?"

"He lost his father recently, and it shook him." Fran recalled the bleakness in his eyes and wished there was something she could do to erase it. "But it's more than that, too. Who knows what. Another difference is, he's working while he's here. He's never done that before."

"That's a shame about his dad." Cinnamon opened the large, stainless-steel refrigerator. "I hope you don't mind that I bought premade salad."

"Not at all," Fran said. "What you said before—I don't want you to wait on me. Please let me help."

"Go ahead and find a salad bowl, then. They're in the cabinet under the mixer. So has he talked about his father or his grief?"

Fran shook her head. "Mitch is a very private man."

For some reason, Cinnamon gave her a canny look. "You *really* like him, don't you?"

"No." An instant later Fran sighed. "All right, I do have a crush on him. But nothing will come of that, and he'll never know. We're friends. Now, I don't want to discuss Mitch anymore," she said, emptying the greens into the bowl. "I want to talk about you. I haven't even heard about your childbirth class."

"This is week three, and it's really fun." Cinnamon set the table and filled Fran in on interesting details, which included practicing relaxation techniques with Nick. "Best of all, every woman in class looks as big as I do. We're all losing our belly buttons and can barely see our feet. And look at my breasts! They've grown a full size. Naturally, Nick likes that. Plus—" she lowered her voice "—I can't get enough sex." She gave a wicked grin. "He likes that, too."

Fran laughed as she added tongs to the salad bowl. "I imagine he would."

Still smiling, Cinnamon shook her head and turned on the heat to steam the beans. "The truth is, I'm happier than I've ever been. Sometimes I pinch myself to make sure this isn't a dream." A funny expression crossed her face and she glanced in wonder at her belly, which suddenly looked lopsided. "Look, she's kicking. Here, feel." She laid Fran's palm over the baby. "That's her foot."

Now the ache in her heart was back. Fran hadn't been pregnant long enough to feel life. Awed, she bit her lip. "That's amazing." Tears filled her eyes. "You're so lucky."

"Oh, honey." Cinnamon made a sympathetic face. "You're remembering your pregnancy, aren't you?"

Unable to lie, Fran nodded and swiped her eyes. "That doesn't mean I'm not overjoyed for you and Nick." She managed a smile. "I am."

"I know." Her friend squeezed her hand. "And I also know that someday we'll both get to feel *your* baby kick."

Since Fran wasn't about to get pregnant without a husband, she wasn't so sure about that.

"I didn't think I'd ever get married, either, remember? You'll find the right man, I know it. Then you'll make a baby."

For some reason, Fran's thoughts turned to Mitch, who changed girlfriends the way she changed aprons. He was her friend, and not the marrying kind. And she really didn't want to think about him anymore tonight.

"Enough about me. You said on the phone that Nick finished the nursery. When do I get to see it?"

"How about right now, while we're waiting for the steaks."

They walked up the wide, lushly carpeted steps, past the spacious master suite and the guest bedroom where Nick's almost fifteen-year-old niece, Abby, sometimes stayed. At the end of the hall was a third room painted rosy pink. White ruffled curtains softened the big window and a mural of colorful zoo animals filled one wall.

Fran admired the animals, painted by the multitalented Nick. She turned to the crib, which was a true work of art. "This is the most beautiful crib I've ever seen." Unable to resist, she ran her hands over the smooth, polished cherrywood.

"Nick made that," Cinnamon said with pride.

"Wow. Maybe he should start a crib-making business. He'd make a fortune." Which he'd already done several times with his clever inventions. The cranberry sorter he'd designed was used in factories across the country.

"He just might do that. But, if he doesn't, I know he'll make one for you when your time comes."

"Steaks are ready," Nick called out from downstairs.

"Finally." Cinnamon licked her lips and rubbed her hands together.

Fran was hungry, too. And dearly in need of a good time. No more talk of finding Mr. Right or having a baby of her own or anything so serious. The rest of the evening was for eating, laughing and figuring out what food to serve at the shower.

To prove it, she laughed and grabbed Cinnamon's arm. "Let's eat."

DESPITE THE restful shush of the ocean through the slider he'd cracked open, Mitch couldn't sleep. Here it was, midnight, and his mind refused to shut down. Unfortunately, not one of his racing thoughts was remotely connected to the book he needed to finish.

Sex usually emptied his brain and relaxed him enough to fall asleep. What he craved tonight was heat, the kind that burned through a man until he was mindless with it and every part of him smoldered. What was it like to experience that kind of passion? He'd always held back in his relationships to protect himself, since letting go completely left a man weak and vulnerable—another lesson drummed into him by his father.

But tonight he was so very cold, with a chill not even his down comforter could thaw. At the moment, he'd sell his soul to the devil for a passionate woman to hold on to.

Through the window he'd left open in the bathroom, he heard the crunch of gravel. Soft light from the motion-sensitive outdoor lights bathed the room.

Fran was back. She'd stayed out late. Certainly not at Cinnamon's. Pregnant women needed extra sleep, didn't they? Fran must have been out with someone else.

The stab of jealousy was swift and unexpected. She'd said she wasn't dating anyone. So where had she gone?

Mitch frowned into the darkness. What the hell business was it of his? Outside of friendship, he had no claims on Fran. If she lived in Seattle, he might date her. But Fran wouldn't be the same without her B and B—and he wasn't here to think about dating her. Or anything else. Yet, he couldn't help wishing that she'd rush upstairs and join him in bed.

Not gonna happen. Muttering a string of foul words, he punched his pillow, then rolled onto his stomach. He would shut off his mind and sleep. *Now.* He closed his eyes.

Through sheer will, he managed a few hours in fits and starts. Before dawn his brain began to hum with mindless chatter and he gave up.

Breakfast wasn't for hours yet, but he needed caffeine. The suite didn't come with a coffeemaker, but yesterday Fran had said to help himself to anything in the kitchen. With coffee and luck, by breakfast he'd have written a page or two. A bout of creativity would do wonders for his low spirits.

He pulled on a pair of sweats and a T-shirt. Yawning and combing his hair with his fingers, he wandered barefoot down the stairs.

To his surprise, the kitchen lights were on, along with the radio. Sounded like a news program. Fran was awake. The two of them up when most people were still in bed felt intimate. Special. Until he wondered why she hadn't slept in. Maybe she'd met someone last night and was too keyed up.

He hoped not, because he sure as hell was not in the mood to hear about that. He hesitated and almost went back upstairs. But the whole downstairs smelled of fresh coffee, and he couldn't resist.

He padded across the carpet, stopping by the bookcase, just beyond where the light touched the dining room. From here, he could see the colorful kitchen. Fran's back was to him. Thanks to the radio, she didn't hear him and he was able to watch her unobserved.

Wearing bright, striped socks, dressed in a teal blue T-shirt, chocolate-brown cords and a bib apron, she peered at an open cookbook propped up beside a large mixing bowl. Her braid was tucked inside the apron bow at the small of her back. This allowed him a decent view of her waist and round hips. Even more appealing were her sure, confident movements as she measured ingredients and stirred.

Once, Mitch had taken his own confidence for granted. Now he envied Fran hers. While he stood there watching like a voyeur, she turned the bowl upside down onto a clean cloth, then brushed her hands together.

Time to announce his presence. He cleared his throat. "'Morning."

She whirled toward him, her eyes wide with surprise. "Good morning. You're up early."

"So are you. Couldn't sleep, huh?"

"I've always been an early riser. And I wanted to get started on breakfast." She tugged her braid free.

"Seems a waste of your time to do all that work for one person."

"We already discussed this. You're a guest here and that entitles you to a full breakfast. Besides, I like cooking for you."

The words and the sweet light in her eyes were exactly what he needed. But, even as he soaked up her warmth like a dry sponge, the devil prodded him to say, "Even when you're out past midnight?"

Her eyes narrowed a fraction. "How did you know that?"

Tension knotted the back of his neck, and he silently condemned himself for making the crack. He shrugged. "Heard you drive up."

"But your lights were out." Looking contrite, she frowned. "I meant to be quiet. If I woke you, I'm sorry."

She'd noticed his lights were out? For some reason, he liked that. "It's not your fault I can't sleep."

"Is there anything I can do?"

Oh, yeah, but he wasn't about to go near that loaded question. He shook his head. "There's a lot on my mind."

Understanding bloomed on her face and he knew she wouldn't pry, even if she wanted to. That was her way, and he was grateful. Yet, it took every ounce of will to hold back his own questions. He wanted to know where she'd been and who she'd spent her evening with. He decided to draw her out over breakfast.

"Breakfast won't be ready until eight," she said. "But, if you're hungry, there's plenty to snack on in the fridge."

He shook his head. "Figured I'd work a few hours. I came down to get coffee before I settled in."

"Of course. I should have thought of that." She took a mug from the cabinet, set it on the counter and filled it. "I'll pick up a coffeemaker for you later today so you won't have to come all the way downstairs next time."

"I don't mind," he said, the thought of seeing her first thing in the morning cheering his sorry ass way too much. "But a Thermos for later in the day would be great. I'll reimburse you, of course." He cupped the mug, feeling the heat of the liquid through the ceramic.

"All right, I'll pick one up today." She glanced at the clock. "I'd better get back to making this yeast bread, or you won't eat until noon."

He carried his coffee upstairs, already looking forward to seeing her again.

FRAN HAD JUST SET OUT a small pitcher of juice when Mitch crossed the entry. The pepper bacon seemed to want to burn this morning and needed a watchful eye. Even so, her gaze fixed on him.

Since she'd last seen him, he'd showered and combed his hair, and the gray sweats, black T-shirt and bare feet had been replaced by faded jeans, a dark green turtleneck and sneakers. He hadn't shaved and she had an impulse to rub her hand over his rough check.

Oh, she liked this man. For the second time today, her heart gave a joyous kick. Last night, she'd admitted her crush to Cinnamon and that she considered Mitch a friend. The friend part was true, but her feelings ran deeper than a shallow crush. She was very attracted to Mitch. She simply couldn't help herself.

As he drew closer, she offered a welcoming smile. "Good morning, again."

"Now that it's breakfast time, it is." Looking genuinely glad to see her, he grinned.

Afraid her face might reflect her feelings, she focused on stabbing bacon strips and laying them on paper towels to drain. "It's a good thing you're hungry, because I've cooked you a feast."

"My stomach thanks you in advance."

Smiling again, she gestured at the table. "Please, sit down."

"You didn't set a place for yourself."

"You know I don't eat with my guests," Fran replied as she sliced the fresh-from-the-oven yeast bread. She'd eaten hours ago, while waiting for the bread to rise.

"Yeah, but, since I'm the only one here, I figured... No big deal."

His obvious disappointment tugged at her heart. The man was alone most of the day and evening. Everybody needed human contact. She'd shared wine and cheese with the Hortons because they'd invited her to. Why not sit with Mitch in the morning?

"If you want company, I'm happy to sit with you."

"I do."

The timer pinged, and she pivoted toward the stove.

"What can I do to help this morning?" Mitch asked.

"Relax and sit down."

She slipped her hands into a pair of red oven mitts and opened the oven door to take out the frittata. Heat rushed out, and the redolent fragrances of basil and dill mingled with the aromas of bacon and bread. Even though she wasn't hungry, her mouth watered.

When she turned, Mitch was standing at the serving counter. "What?" she asked.

"It makes me uncomfortable when you wait on me."

"You never minded before." She carried the dish to the dining room table.

"I should have. I'll bring in the basket of bread and the bacon." He licked his lips. "Are you trying to fatten me up?"

It was good to see the teasing twinkle in his eye. "Maybe." She smiled. "Believe it or not, I halved the frittata recipe. But don't worry about leftovers. The gulls will happily finish whatever you don't."

As if they'd overheard, Stubby and Stumpy swooped low and landed on the railing in front of the slider. Beyond them, the clouds racing by promised fickle weather.

"I'd best not overeat, then. They might get excited, and not in a good way." Mitch gestured Fran into the chair across from him.

Once she sat down, he took his own seat. She cut the frittata and served him a generous slice.

He helped himself to bread and four strips of bacon. "Sure you don't want to share the feast?"

She shook her head.

"You're really missing out," he said, chewing with gusto. "This is delicious."

For a while, he was silent, eating like a starving man. Whatever put the shadows in his eyes hadn't dampened his appetite.

When he finally came up for air, he wiped his mouth. "Do you know a man named Foster Gravis?"

"He's a local artist who lives a mile or two from here. When aunt Frannie was alive, he used to stop by now and then for coffee. Why?"

"I met him yesterday on the beach." He looked both guilty and defensive, as if he were admitting to a crime.

"He was looking for driftwood, so I helped him find what he wanted."

This didn't surprise Fran. "Probably getting ready for the Cranberry Festival. We put up a big, heated tent for the local artists to sell their wares."

"I offered to buy one of the pieces in his yard. He turned me down—said none of it was for sale." Mitch scratched his head and looked mystified. "I'm sure he needed the money."

"Those things have been there for years. He's attached to them. But he'll have plenty of pieces to choose from at the Cranberry Festival."

Mitch nodded. "Did you get all those errands done yesterday?"

"Mostly. I have a few more today."

"That must be some to-do list."

"Not really. Some stores are closed on Sunday, so I couldn't go yesterday."

"I didn't realize anything in Cranberry closed, ever."

"Not during the summer. But now that the tourist season has slowed down, there's no reason to stay open seven days a week. Betsy's Yarn Shop is one of those stores. I special-ordered yarn for the receiving blanket I'll be knitting for my godchild, and it should be there today." Knitting the blanket would take up a good chunk of her spare time between now and the shower, a week from Saturday. "There's a new gourmet-chocolate store west of downtown called Alice Caroline's that carries wonderful chocolate, and I want to stop in there, too. I think chocolate will be a nice addition to the cranberry bars, don't you?"

"I sure do." Mitch smacked his lips. "When you're ready to test that new and improved recipe, don't forget, I'm your man."

She had no objections to that.

"How was dinner last night?" he asked.

"Great. You should see Cinnamon. She's enormous and still has two months to go."

"I'll bet carrying that baby around makes her tired. Do anything interesting after you left her place?"

He lifted and drained a glass of cranberry juice as easy as you please, but a fine tension stiffened his shoulders.

Puzzled, Fran frowned. "Why do you ask?"

He shrugged. "Just wondered what or who kept you out so late last night."

His slightly narrowed eyes gleamed sharply—a jealous look.

Impossible. How could Mitch be jealous of whom she spent her evenings with? No, she was imagining things. "Cinnamon and I never get the chance to visit anymore, and last night was the perfect time."

Nick had turned in at eleven, but Cinnamon had wanted to stay up later. They'd planned the menu for the shower—among other things Cinnamon wanted some of Alice Caroline's candies—then, just as they always did when they had the time, they'd talked about anything and everything. Except Mitch. "We had a ball."

"Good for you." Looking far more at ease, Mitch laced his hands behind his head. "I envy you women for the close relationships you form with each other."

"You wrote a book about that."

"So I did."

While Mitch pulled the frittata dish toward his plate and cut himself seconds, Fran topped off their coffees. "Speaking of books, you said you wanted to write a few pages before breakfast. Did you have enough time?"

"Pretty much," he said without quite meeting her eyes.

It was as if he were hiding something. But what? As greatly as Fran wanted answers, she refused to pry. If Mitch wanted to talk about his—

"You don't believe me."

He sounded irritated and accusing. Fran bristled. "Geesh, you're touchy. Of course I do. Why wouldn't I?"

A few seconds of taut silence passed before he stabbed his hand through his hair. "You're right, I over-reacted. Sometimes when I'm writing I get weird."

That explained it. Instantly, she relaxed. "You sound like a man badly in need of chocolate. Why don't I pick you up some of Alice Caroline's handmade candies. What's your favorite kind?"

"Anything with nuts and caramel. How much do you need?" Mitch raised his hip and extracted his wallet.

"Not a penny. You're skipping the wine and cheese, and I want to do *some*thing. This is my treat."

"All right." He returned the wallet to his rear pocket, propped his chin on his palm and studied her. "Tell me, Fran, how do you think people find their bliss?"

It was an interesting question. "That's what your book's about, or am I wrong?"

"You're right."

"Then, why are you asking me?"

"Why shouldn't I ask you? I value your opinion."

This sounded like the man she knew, and was exactly

the sort of discussion he'd start over breakfast. "I suppose a person finds her bliss by loving her work."

He nodded and stroked his stubble with long fingers. "What do you mean, love your work?"

This was vintage Mitch Matthews. Uncertain what she could say that Mitch didn't already know, Fran hesitated. But the open interest on his face was enough to persuade her.

"Well," she said, fiddling with her braid while she searched for an answer, "I suppose, I mean, you feel passionate about it. You have passion and love for your work. Am I right?"

"Hmm. Are you passionate about your work, Fran?"

His entire focus was pinned on her, as if her opinion mattered more than anything else in the world. How heady that was. Every nerve in her body strained toward him.

She swallowed. "Since taking care of people and cooking are things I love, I'd say so."

At his nod of encouragement, she continued. "But passion and love of your work isn't enough, not for me. I'd like to get married someday and have a few kids." She thought of Cinnamon and Nick, so happy and excited about the baby. "I think if I had my own family *and* my work, I'd know true bliss."

An odd look she didn't understand crossed his face. "You want to finish my book for me?"

She smiled. "That's a good one, Mitch. Ha, ha."

He did not return the smile. Or finish his second helping. "Well, thanks for a great breakfast and your good company. I should get back to work now." He set his napkin beside his plate, then glanced at her. "Unless you'd like help cleaning up?"

Fran shook her head. "Washing dishes may not be my passion, but I don't mind the work. You have more important things to do."

"Right." He pushed back his chair and stood.

Chapter Five

Two hours later, Mitch had written exactly one sentence. Fran's words, modified to fit his style. *We find our bliss by doing work we passionately enjoy, while emotionally and lovingly supported by family and friends.*

Her words had eerily echoed his father's advice. Find a woman to settle down with, have a few kids and put your career second.

That made sense for most people. His thoughts turned to Fran and the way her warmth and enthusiasm were evident in everything she did. She was a good friend, giving solace to his soul. For her, love would come easily.

But for him… Was he even capable of love?

At thirty-seven and without ever having fallen in love, Mitch seriously doubted it. And didn't want to think about that now, not with so much work to do.

He forced his attention on the words he'd typed, which he needed to expand into a full chapter.

And he would, after checking his e-mail. A year ago, Fran had installed Wi-Fi, making that easy. After three days away from the computer there were e-mails from his publicist, his agent and his editor, among others.

Why couldn't they do as he'd asked, and leave him be? He logged off without reading the messages.

Time for another beach walk. Looking forward to the fresh air, he grabbed a sweatshirt, pocketed the key and went downstairs.

Fifteen minutes later, without having intended to, he strode onto Foster Gravis's porch and knocked on the door.

"It's open," Foster called out.

Mitch walked into a small, simply furnished room crammed with raw chunks of wood and completed figures similar to the ones outside, only smaller. Wearing safety glasses and sitting in a faded armchair, with tools spread over a TV table and wood shavings scattered over the braided rug, Foster deftly wielded a chisel over a fist-sized piece of wood.

If he was surprised to see Mitch he didn't let on. He simply nodded and continued to pound a small hammer against the chisel.

"Mind if I watch you work awhile?" Mitch asked.

"Not at all. Grab a pair of glasses." He nodded at a nearby shelf. "Sit on the sofa or bring a chair from the kitchen."

FRAN LOVED Alice Caroline's Gourmet Chocolates, a charming shop located in what had once been a vacation cottage. Armed only with her grandmother's handwritten candy recipes, the sixty-seven-year-old Alice Caroline, a transplant from Palo Alto, had dived into the candy-making business with tireless enthusiasm. The shop had opened seven months ago, a week before Valentine's Day, and business had been brisk ever since. Locals and tourists alike paid premium prices for the hand-crafted candies and the wide selection of imported baking chocolate. Aside from her husband and several part-time clerks, Alice employed a full-time chocolatier and a Webmaster to handle her booming Internet business.

This morning, a knot of people milled around the counter in the main room where Alice and her husband Bert, who had retired from a busy pediatrics practice, cheerfully served them.

Fran decided to put off buying candy until the crowd thinned. She would look over the baking chocolates and select several to test in her cranberry bar recipe. To reach the baking section at the back of the cottage a person walked through a large space filled with small tables for people to enjoy their treats and a cup of coffee.

The instant Fran stepped into the crowded table area, she spied two familiar faces. They saw her, too.

"Yoo-hoo! Fran!" called Noelle and Joelle Sommers, never-married fraternal twins who were nearly eighty.

They once had run a bed-and-breakfast and had mentored Fran during her first year alone in the business, after Aunt Frannie had died. They also were part of the Friday girls, a group of women who met for lunch at Rosy's Diner every other Friday during the off-season.

Except for Cinnamon, every one of the Friday Girls had entered the cook-off, the twins as a team. Competition between the group was friendly but fierce, with no one divulging their food category or any other details. Fran didn't want the twins or anyone else to know about the baking chocolate. If she purchased some, no matter what excuses she made, they might guess.

Stifling a groan—she'd have to come back later to buy it—she smiled, waved and pretended to be here for coffee. As if she hadn't already had more than enough sitting with Mitch at breakfast. She was still puzzled over some of their conversation and the undercurrents she had sensed. But she would sort that out later, when she was alone in her apartment.

She sauntered over. "Hello. How've you two been?"

"Lovely," Joelle said. "Except, we got into a bad habit this summer. Alice Caroline's chocolates are rather addictive. Since May, we've been here every other day."

"Sometimes every single day," Noelle said. "If we don't stop soon, we'll get fat." Winking, she patted her round middle with a gnarled hand.

"Noelle, you are so vain." Behind green-rimmed, rhinestone trifocals—Noelle's were purple—Joelle's grey eyes twinkled. "The boys at the bridge center like us just the way we are, and you know it."

They both hooted as if they'd cracked the funniest joke ever.

"Would you care to join us?" Noelle nodded at the empty café chair at their table for three.

Fran noted their half-empty cups and nearly empty plates. With luck they'd leave soon and she could make her purchases without another trip. "That'd be nice. I'll get my coffee and be right back."

Decaf for her. She moved to the quartet of large Thermoses to one side of the room. Using the honor system, customers paid for their coffee sometime before leaving the shop. Fran would pay later.

When she returned with her mug, Noelle frowned. "Where's your treat?"

"Too early for me."

"It's never too early for chocolate," Joelle said. "You can make coffee at home. If you're not here for the candy, then why are you here?" She eyed Fran shrewdly. "You're not by chance picking up baking chocolate for your cook-off recipe?"

"Maybe she wants candy for someone else." Noelle touched her short, silvery hair and arched her eyebrows. "That nice Mitch Matthews comes to mind."

Fran wasn't surprised she knew about Mitch. The bed-and-breakfast owners were a small enough group that they often knew about each other's guests, especially the famous ones such as Mitch. "You're right, I am picking up chocolate for him," she said.

"I knew it!" Noelle crowed. "Such a fine specimen of a male." She sighed, clasping her hands over her chest.

The twins had met him three years ago when he'd signed books at the local bookstore. Naturally, he'd charmed them with his warmth and attention.

Joelle arched her eyebrows over the rims of her glasses. "Interesting that he's staying with you for five whole weeks."

"And without a girlfriend," Noelle added with a knowing look. "A man who writes such wise books would make a first-rate husband, don't you think?"

"I hadn't thought about that," Fran said. Beyond the fact that things between them never would move in that direction.

"Well, you should," Noelle said.

"Why?" Joelle looked puzzled. "He doesn't seem to stay long with any woman. That's not good husband material."

Noelle tsked. "Only because he hasn't found the right one for him. You're a lovely person, Fran, and he's such a dear, handsome man. I'm hoping the two of you will get together."

She never had been known for her subtlety. "I don't think so. We are friends, though."

Noelle sniffed. "For now. Once you feed him some of Alice Caroline's chocolate, that just might change. They say it stimulates your hormones. And we all know that, once that happens, bye-bye friendship and hello love."

"Noey!" Joelle looked shocked.

Fran choked on her coffee. While heads turned, both women patted her back.

"You can forget about that," she said when she could speak. "As I said, Mitch is my guest and my friend, period."

"All right, but, when that changes, I want to know."

Joelle rammed her sister with her elbow. "You're incorrigible!"

This time, Fran laughed. "There's another reason I'm here." She wouldn't mention the cook-off. "Cinnamon requested the ganache truffles and mint meltaways at her baby shower."

"Heaven in the mouth," Noelle said. "Almost as good as sex."

For a woman well past her prime she certainly enjoyed shocking people. Especially her sister, whose mouth pursed. Pretending she hadn't heard, she turned to Fran. "But the shower isn't for nearly two weeks. Why would you buy the candy so early?"

Noelle's turn to roll her eyes. "Just because you'd eat

it all yourself doesn't mean Fran will. She'll put it into the freezer to keep it fresh, won't you, Fran?" She smiled at Fran. "You look well, dear. I can see that you survived the summer unscathed."

"Aside from several plugged-up toilets and a blown fuse or two," Fran said. "It went by so fast."

"Don't I remember those days," Joelle said. "Wait til you're our age. Then—"

"Time passes even faster," her sister finished. "Only a month left until tourist season is officially over. I'll bet you're glad about that."

"Yes and no," Fran said. "I need a break, but I'll miss the cash flow."

The twins offered matching nods of sympathy.

"Speaking of money," Joelle said, "how's your recipe coming along?"

Fran wasn't about to let on that hers still needed tweaking—a whole lot of it. "It's great. How's yours?"

"Just about perfected." Joelle drank from her large orange cup.

"We bought the cutest layette set for Cinnamon and Nick's baby," Noelle said.

The way she changed the subject made Fran wonder whether their recipe was as far from perfect as hers was.

"It's soft as velvet, covered with little yellow elephants and green giraffes."

"That sounds adorable." Would they ever finish and leave?

"I'll bet you're knitting one of those gorgeous receiving blankets you're so good at making," Joelle said.

"Not yet, but I will be. Betsy special-ordered the

yarn, and it was supposed to arrive this morning. As soon as I leave here, I'll pick it up."

Betsy Tiber, who was Fran and Cinnamon's age and also a member of the Friday Girls, owned the only knitting shop in town. She was lucky enough to be happily married and raising two adorable kids. Fran had a hunch Betsy was living her bliss. How she envied her.

Looking as if she had a secret to share, Joelle beckoned Fran close. "Word on the street is," she said in a low voice, "Betsy's entry in the cook-off will be in the main course category. A chicken cranberry casserole."

"We heard it from Myrtle Stokes at the bridge center," Noelle added in an equally low voice. "Her daughter was in the yarn shop the other day and actually saw a printout of the recipe just lying there by the cash register. Chicken and cranberries." She wrinkled her nose. "Doesn't sound very original, does it?"

Originality was one criteria for winning. Another stipulated that the recipe must include cranberries. The judges would critique the taste, texture and appearance, as well as unusual ingredients.

"Whereas, ours is totally unique," Joelle said. "I imagine yours is, too."

It would be, once Fran figured out the right mix of ingredients. Not about to divulge a thing, she gave a secretive smile. "You'll have to wait and see."

"She's a sneaky one, isn't she?" Noelle teased.

"No more than we are. Tell us, Fran, have you seen the nursery?"

Fran nodded. She told them about the mural and the crib Nick had made.

"A new little angel to spoil." Joelle sighed sweetly. "And you, her godparent. Isn't it exciting?"

"I can't wait!"

"You know," Noelle said, "Cinnamon wasn't looking to meet anyone when she came here."

Joelle nodded. "Exactly. She wasn't even planning to stay in town. And look what happened."

To Fran's relief, she popped the last of her chocolate marshmallow scotchie into her mouth. Now, if only Noelle would finish. But she was too busy talking.

"And it all happened at the Oceanside," she said. "You serve romantic breakfasts and allow people to hold their weddings in your great room. With that view your home is made for romance. It could happen to you, too. You never know." She took a bite of her dwindling coconut almond chocolate bar and eyed Fran.

Fran sipped her coffee so she wouldn't have to respond. Cinnamon had said much the same thing last night. But Fran pretty much *did* know. Each year she was single, the number of decent, available men dropped. Especially here in Cranberry, where there weren't exactly hordes to begin with. If she hadn't taken eight years to get over the last heartache, she would've had more choices.

By the time she set down her cup, Noelle had finished the rest of her dessert. *Finally.* Fran heaved a mental sigh of relief.

"This has been great fun, Fran, but our bridge lesson starts soon, and I'm sure you want to pick up that yarn. Otherwise you'll never finish that blanket before the shower."

Fran stood and collected the dishes. "I'll see you two at the shower."

"And, after that, the cook-off," Joelle said. "Less than a month to go. May the best recipe win."

"THANKS FOR THE COFFEE and the company, Mitch." Foster pulled off his safety glasses, set down his latest work in progress and stood, stretching his arms over his head. "Enjoyed yakking your ear off."

Over the past week Mitch had gotten into the habit of a brisk walk and a stop at Foster's with a Thermos of Fran's coffee. Fran didn't know—for some reason, he didn't want to share this—and he intended to pick up more of the brand she used to pay her back.

"I like your stories," Mitch said, meaning it.

Especially since, beyond an occasional comment, he didn't have to say much. He continued to be amazed at the magic Foster created with his chisels and carving knives while he talked.

Mitch had learned about the artist's long-dead wife and about a much smaller Cranberry thirty years ago. He knew that Foster lived simply out of choice, not necessity, and that his art was an expression of his love of wildlife. Since that first day Foster hadn't mentioned teaching Mitch to carve, but he understood that the offer stood.

At the door, Foster frowned at the dark sky. "We're in for a real downpour. You'd better move it, Mitch."

"See ya," Mitch said. Then he strode out.

His sneakers churned up sand as he quickly made for the Oceanside. As always, after a walk and visit with Foster, he bounded up the stairs of the Oceanside feeling invigorated, his mind sharp and clear. Exactly the mental state he needed to write the book. Not that he'd accomplished much. He'd been here ten days and had written all of fifteen pages. Not nearly enough.

If only he could work as easily as Foster. Dammit, today he would. Setting his jaw, he wiped his feet on the welcome mat, dug his key from his pocket and let himself in the front door. From here, he couldn't see the kitchen, but the Norah Jones song floating toward him told him Fran was back. She'd been out when he left the house, but then she often ran errands, met friends and did whatever Cranberry Festival volunteers did. That she was home shouldn't have cheered him as it did, but the Oceanside seemed lifeless without her.

Leaving his sandy shoes outside and with the empty Thermos in hand, he padded silently toward the kitchen.

Bowls, measuring cups, spoons and various spices and food staples were spread across the counter between the stove and sink. Sitting at the kitchen table, Fran studied a sheet of paper and tapped a ballpoint pen over slightly pursed lips. With the lines of concentration between her eyebrows she looked cute.

"What are you studying so intently?" he asked.

Her head jerked up. "For a big man, you sure can sneak up on a person." She switched off the small CD-radio on the table, her gaze darting over him. "You've been walking the beach quite a bit lately. With your coffee."

"The fresh air keeps my head clear for writing."

Her cheeks went pink and he knew he sounded defensive. After setting the Thermos in the sink he spoke in a gentler voice. "Tweaking the cranberry bar recipe again?"

She nodded.

He'd tasted several of her half-dozen tasty attempts, offering his opinion.

"How's it going?" he asked.

"So-so. I'm wondering what to cut and what to add, besides chocolate, to improve it."

Though she hadn't started the actual cooking process today, Mitch swore he smelled vanilla. His stomach growled, reminding him about lunch. "I'm about to order take-out. Want anything?"

She shook her head. "I bought bread and cold cuts this morning. If you want a sandwich—"

"I don't expect lunch," he said. "And I don't mind ordering out. It's what I do at home, and what I've been doing since I got here."

"I should have said something sooner. There's always plenty to eat right here. Since I'll be fixing myself a sandwich soon, it's no bother to make enough for two."

Appealing as the offer was, she already cooked for him every morning. "Tell you what, I'll make the sandwiches and reimburse you for the food."

She opened her mouth but he stopped her with a gesture. "No arguments. Let me wash up, then I'll get started. And maybe later, you'll let me taste-test that new recipe."

"Okay, but it may not be ready for hours. I don't want to bother you while you're working."

He appreciated her thoughtfulness and decided to wash up, make them both sandwiches, eat his upstairs and leave her alone to tinker with her recipe.

Yet, minutes later, he handed Fran her plate, pulled out a bar stool and sat down at the serving counter.

Chapter Six

Fran finished the ham and Swiss cheese sandwich Mitch had made for her and thought about changes to the cranberry bar recipe.

Or tried. Concentrating wasn't easy, not with Mitch a mere eight feet away. He wasn't doing anything to distract her—simply eating the last of his lunch and reading the latest edition of the *Cranberry News Weekly*, which was printed and delivered every Tuesday.

A long-sleeve rugby shirt stretched across his broad shoulders. His hair was wind-tousled and his face ruddy from the brisk sea air. Oh, what a gorgeous, sexy man.

The counter hid the rest of him, but Fran knew that snug jeans showcased his long, powerful legs and the bulge behind his zipper...

Desire and strong emotions she didn't want to feel made her own legs weak. Thank goodness he couldn't read her mind! Feeling unsettled, she crumpled her napkin and silently urged him to go away so that she could focus.

Yet, confusingly, despite her private agitation, the silence between them was not uncomfortable. Fran actually liked the way the kitchen felt with Mitch here. And, anyway, he'd leave soon enough, to work on his book.

As a subtle hint that it was time to get busy, she stood, picked up her plate and collected his. "That was a good sandwich. Thanks."

"Anytime."

She loaded the dishes into the dishwasher. Surely he'd leave now. But he seemed in no hurry. He gestured at the half-finished receiving blanket she'd left on the love seat in the great room, visible beyond the bookcase. "That the baby blanket you mentioned?"

Fran nodded. "I thought I'd work on it while the cranberry bars bake."

"I admire people who work with their hands. Foster. And you, knitting *and* cooking." He gave his head an I'm-impressed shake. "A woman of many talents."

Looking as if he planned to sit awhile, he rifled through the paper—it wasn't a big paper, so what was taking him so long?—while she mixed ingredients for a new batch of bars.

Why didn't he leave? she wondered as she hand-chopped thick chunks of the bittersweet chocolate she'd bought at Alice Caroline's. She'd tried milk chocolate and unsweetened and hadn't been thrilled with either. The chocolate smelled heavenly. Unable to resist a taste, Fran popped a chunk into her mouth. The rich flavor burst on her tongue, and she let out a soft moan of pleasure.

Mitch glanced at her mouth with veiled eyes and an unreadable expression. "That good, huh?"

"It is. Last week when you asked about my bliss, I forgot to mention chocolate."

"Chocolate and bliss," he said with a thoughtful nod. "Brilliant."

"Brilliant? How so?"

"Eating chocolate is a metaphor for enjoying the simple things in life. A piece of quality chocolate. The sun on your back." He smiled warmly. "Sharing lunch in a good friend's kitchen."

Fran returned the smile. She was glad he thought of her as a friend, even if her feelings went beyond the boundaries of friendship. Mitch would never know.

"Would you like to try some?" she asked. "It isn't as sweet as the candy you had last week, but it's wonderful, all the same. Here." She cut a generous chunk from the large bar.

Mitch leaned across the counter and opened his mouth. She fed him like a lover, her fingers brushing his warm, soft lips. Only, she wasn't his lover.

His eyes went dark and hot. Heat licked through Fran. This was dangerous, yet it was all she could do to pull her hand away.

Flustered and unnerved, she spun toward the sink to wash her hands. She took her time, running the tepid water over her skin until she felt reasonably composed, and continued to puzzle over what seemed to be growing between her and Mitch. Since that first night, he hadn't touched her and, until today, hadn't shot her one sexual look.

If only he'd go away and leave her alone. Shouldn't he be working? Not about to ask—what he did with his afternoon was none of her business and, besides, any mention of the book made him testy—she added four beaten eggs to her mixing bowl, stirring by hand. Apparently writing books was a touchy business.

Fran didn't glance Mitch's way again until she had measured the flour and sugar, but she felt his gaze. "Um, I need to concentrate and you're distracting me," she said, reaching for the salt. "Why don't I leave a plate outside your door later?"

Of course, then she wouldn't get his immediate reaction to this recipe. But at least he'd leave.

"I'd rather sit here and wait," he said, looking as if his own words surprised him. "I want to see your passion and enthusiasm at work. I won't say another word."

So that was the reason for his avid interest. Research. Fran was disappointed but also relieved. Even so, her whole body went on alert and she could barely focus. Which was silly. Food Network people would be watching her work at the cook-off, and this was good practice.

"It's all right if you talk," she said, marveling at how normal she sounded. "But trust me, measuring and stirring isn't exactly exciting. While you sit here, maybe you'll think up a clever name for the bars."

"I'll mull that over."

Suddenly rain pummeled the beach, loud even through the glass and bouncing on the deck like little bullets. With the rain and Mitch sitting here, the room felt cozier than ever.

As she sprinkled dried cranberries into the bowl, Mitch studied her through hooded eyes.

"What you said about measuring and stirring— you're wrong. Even now I can sense your passion."

The air between them seemed to sizzle. At least for Fran. She swallowed. "Can you?"

"Can't *you?*"

"I suppose." Acutely self-conscious, she added a pinch of cayenne to add a surprise burst of heat, then Dutch processed cocoa and finally the chocolate chunks.

If only he'd stop looking at her and making her want what she never could have, a relationship beyond friendship. The only thing to do was bring his work into the conversation. "Last week you asked me about bliss, but you never said whether you agree with me."

Well, *that* wiped the heat from his eyes. "I agree with every word."

"Okay, but how do *you* think people find their bliss?"

His face closed. "You want to know that, you'll have to read the book."

The surly reply stung. "Fine." She pulled a glass pan from a cabinet under the counter. "I have a recipe to perfect, so please go away."

MITCH KNEW he'd hurt Fran. What a dolt. He wasn't leaving until he apologized. "I shouldn't have snapped at you."

In the process of greasing the pan, she looked up, frowning. "No, you shouldn't have. It was a harmless question." She poured batter into the pan, then carried it to the oven. "Sometimes I wonder, Mitch. I really do."

"What's that supposed to mean?"

She didn't answer until the stuff was in the oven and the timer set. She turned toward him, hands on her hips and eyes flashing. "You're supposed to be Mr. Positive, the guy who motivates people. Yet, since you got here ten days ago, you've been touchy, abrupt and sometimes downright rude. I realize you lost your father, and I'm sorry about that. But you need a big-time attitude adjustment."

He'd never seen her like this, and felt about two feet tall for provoking her. Yet, in an odd way, her anger felt right. He needed and deserved it.

"You're not telling me anything I don't know," he said, rubbing the back of his neck. "I've been a real jerk, and I apologize."

For all of two seconds, her lips remained tightly closed. Then she sighed and leaned against the sink, arms over her chest. "Accepted."

"Sometimes authors write books to figure out the answer to a question. That's what I'm doing. It's challenging." Admitting that he knew squat about bliss was daunting and hard, but she deserved to know.

"I never realized." Her expression softened further. "Thank you for explaining."

Why he wanted to kiss her now was beyond him. But he did, even more than when she'd fed him chocolate. Then the feel of her fingers as they grazed his lips and the undisguised need in her eyes had all but burned right through his self-control. She wasn't touching him now. But talking this way warmed his heart and soul in ways he didn't understand.

"There is one thing I know for sure. This conversation, watching you—it's all good. You're helping me find the answers I need."

"Really?"

A pleased expression lit up her face, transforming her into the most beautiful, desirable woman he'd ever seen. Hardly aware of his actions, he slid off the stool.

"There's more," he said, rounding the counter and advancing toward her. "Something I just now realized."

"What's that?" She stayed where she was, her expression subtly shifting from satisfaction to sexual awareness, her hands behind her, gripping the edge of the sink.

"You inspire me."

She swallowed. "That's quite a compliment."

Inches away from her, he stopped. "Trouble is, right now it's hard to concentrate." He cupped her face and looked deeply into her eyes. "All I think about is kissing you."

Letting go of the counter, she wrapped her arms around his neck. "Then do it."

FRAN FELT SOFT and warm in Mitch's arms, sweeter than he'd ever dreamed. He meant to keep this first kiss light and teasing, but her lips were eager and yielding and he wanted her so badly. He claimed her mouth in a hard, yearning demand for more that seemed to fuel her own need as her fingers threaded through his hair, urging him closer.

It wasn't enough. He deepened the kiss, tangling his tongue with hers. She tasted of chocolate. The passion he craved was there, too, simmering and impatient. She pressed closer, wriggling her curves seductively against him, threatening to burn every thought from his mind.

But he was the product of his father, a man of control. He broke contact, his breathing hard. Her eyelids fluttered open. Her lips were red from his kisses and she looked dazed.

Mitch was a little dazed himself. She'd given him a

glimpse into paradise. He wanted more, but wasn't about to take it. To keep from reaching for her again he curled his hands into fists. "I'd best get out of here."

Hugging herself, she nodded. "Do you think you can concentrate now?"

"I'll damn well try."

The timer pinged.

"The cranberry bars. I almost forgot." Red tinged her cheeks.

Despite the amazing aroma filling the kitchen, so had Mitch.

"Hold on, and I'll give you one to take upstairs," she said. "You can let me know what you think tomorrow at breakfast."

Mitch waited while she cut him a steaming square, both of them silent with what had happened.

"You'll want to wait til this cools."

He needed to cool off, too. A thought that made his mouth quirk. "Thanks."

He headed upstairs, hard and aching, but happier than he'd been in a long time. For the first time in months, he was on fire. At the moment, that was enough.

Chapter Seven

The waffle iron was sizzling hot, the sausages were cooked and keeping warm in the oven and the coffee was fresh. Now if only Mitch showed up. In the time he'd been here, he hadn't missed one breakfast.

Fran shot an anxious glance at the wall clock. Almost eight thirty, well past the time she always served. She had errands to run and baking to do. Another batch of cranberry bars.

Her fidgety hands stirred the waffle batter, which was starting to separate. Where was he? If he didn't show up in five minutes, she'd leave his food in the oven with a note.

She totally understood that he might be uncomfortable to face her, even if he *had* enjoyed those kisses. She wasn't exactly relaxed herself. She was... nervous.

A grown woman, apprehensive of the man who had thoroughly kissed her! Brushing a lock of hair from her face, she scoffed at herself, but that didn't dispel the tension that hummed through her veins. To be held and kissed by the man she cared deeply for had made her feel edgy and hungry and also wonderful. An unforgettable glimpse of heaven.

Mitch didn't know, would never know, the depth of her feelings. As long as she kept them to herself, there was nothing to worry about.

The danger lay in her physical need for him, which had grown more intense and harder to contain. Even though he wasn't the settling-down kind, she easily could give herself completely to him. But, if she did, she wasn't sure she could bear the pain when he left.

She'd experienced that kind of anguish once, when Leif had walked out of her life after the miscarriage. Losing him and her dream of a family of her own... well, she wasn't about to intentionally expose herself to any more heartache.

At last, there he was, padding barefoot across the hallway in jeans and a long-sleeve navy T-shirt, his hair wet and combed back, his jaw shaved. Fran liked that he'd left off his socks, which seemed oddly intimate and trusting. But then, if he'd worn heavy boots she'd have liked that, too.

Oh, she had a wicked-bad case of lovesickness. Stifling a sigh she filled a mug and placed it on the serving counter. "Good morning."

"'Morning." His voice sounded rusty, as if he'd just awakened, and his eyes lit with appreciation as they combed over her. "Boy, do I need this coffee."

She smiled, glad that she'd taken extra care with her clothes and makeup and relieved that she'd recently brushed her teeth. Because by the look on his face he would kiss her again. Soon.

She certainly wouldn't stop him, which was utterly

confusing, since kisses would lead exactly where she should not go. Her heart pounded and her body strained toward him.

Ignoring her feelings, she opened the hot waffle iron. Batter hissed and bubbled as she ladled it onto the iron. "I wasn't sure you'd make it to breakfast."

"I worked late last night."

He looked and sounded pleased. Happy for him and proud that she inspired him, Fran smiled. "Then, the book is going well?"

"Not bad. Thanks for waiting on breakfast for me. If I'm keeping you from something, go."

"Grocery shopping and a trip to the printer's to pick up some promotional posters to show everyone at tonight's meeting for the Cranberry Festival. The errands will keep. Tell me, what did you think of the cranberry bars?"

"They were good," he said, sipping from the mug. "I liked the crunch and the bite of spice. What about you? Are you happy with them?"

"I think I overcooked them a bit." But then, she'd been a tad distracted by Mitch's kisses. "And I'm not sure I like the bittersweet chocolate."

"What about milk chocolate?"

"I tried that before. It was overly sweet. That's why I switched to the bittersweet."

"You could use both."

"That's not a bad idea. I'll try that. Your waffle will be ready soon. Why don't you sit down and enjoy your fruit salad?"

Rubbing his hands together, he took his place at the table, spooned himself a large bowl of fruit and devoured it. "That was great," he said when the bowl was empty.

"You finished just in time for the main course." Wearing oven mitts, she brought him two waffles and a plate of sausages. "These dishes are hot, so be careful," she warned as she set both fragrant dishes in front of him.

"I like hot."

Gazing at her mouth he shot her a smoldering look that left no doubt of his meaning. It was all she could do to keep from melting at his feet.

"There are two kinds of syrup," she said, slipping off the oven mitts to snatch both from the middle of the table. "Maple and blueberry."

Mitch took the syrup from her hands, then caught her wrists. His dark eyes searched her face. "Sooner or later, I mean to kiss you again."

As much as she wanted and had hoped for that, suddenly she changed her mind. Fearful of getting hurt, she pulled away. "I don't think we should."

"Why not? We both enjoyed it."

He stared at her mouth, and she swore her lips tingled. "I've had time to think about things. Kissing you again is a bad idea."

"Mind telling me why?"

"You'll be leaving in a few weeks, and I'm not good at short-term affairs." Avoiding his gaze she grabbed the oven mitts.

"I realize that, but, after yesterday, I thought… You should've stopped me."

She'd wanted him too much for that. "I know."

Unable to bear his searching look—what if he guessed her true feelings?—she returned the mitts to the kitchen. "I'd better feed the gulls. They've been waiting a while."

Silence fell between them, broken only by the clatter of the serving spoon against the Melmac plates. As Fran carried the gulls' breakfast toward the deck, Mitch jumped up to open the slider for her.

A glance at the gulls and he frowned. "Looks like Stumpy's other leg went gimpy."

For the first time that morning, Fran truly looked at the bird. To her dismay, his normally smooth feathers were ruffled and he couldn't stand. She had no idea how he'd managed to land.

"He's hurt." She set the plates on the deck, then hurried to the wall phone in the kitchen. "I'm calling the vet."

Tess and Bill Martin were a fortysomething husband-and-wife vet team. Both handled domestic animals, but Tess also worked with the wild ones.

Minutes later, Fran hung up. She returned to the slider. "They said to bring Stumpy right over."

"You're taking a wild bird to the vet?" Mitch's incredulous expression was almost comical.

And maddening. Fran stiffened. "Why wouldn't I? He's a living creature who needs my help."

She fished through the drawer for the small bottle of mild sedative tablets Tess had given her when she'd brought Stubby in last year after he lost his appetite, in case she needed to bring him back.

Looking chastised, Mitch nodded. "You're right. What can I do?"

She found the bottle and popped the top. "I'm going to grab an old blanket and get the cage out of the basement. Don't let him leave."

His eyebrows shot up. "Uh, just how do I keep him here?"

"If he finishes his food, offer him more sausage.

First, though, take one of these pills—it's a mild sedative—and hide it in his bite."

Mitch nodded, and she raced down the basement stairs for the carrying cage Nick Mahoney had fashioned for just this situation.

When she returned, the birds still were eating. Not five feet away, Mitch was hunkered down in the threshold of the slider, holding out a sausage. They ignored him.

There was something sweet about the big man trying to tempt the birds. Fran set the cumbersome cage on the floor behind him.

"Thank you." Without a thought for what she was doing she touched his solid shoulder. His strength and heat warmed her palm—and the rest of her.

"Easiest work I've ever done."

He grinned up at her, the unfettered emotion in his eyes so intense, she caught her breath. She knew she should move away, yet her hand lingered on his shoulder.

His grin faded and his eyes darkened, the smoldering hunger on his face touching her like a caress.

Her body began to thrum. She could easily bend down and lose herself in him.

"Sure you don't want to kiss me?"

She jerked back her hand, then stepped away from him. "I'm sure. Um, thanks for trying to feed Stumpy the sausage. I'd better give it to him instead."

"Okay." Mitch cleared his throat, stood and handed her the sausage. "What else can I do?"

"You can bring me the blanket and cage when I need them. Meantime, please, sit down and finish your breakfast before it gets cold."

"And miss this? No way." He grabbed his plate from the table and ate standing.

Fran moved the cage close to the threshold of the deck, leaving it inside so as not to frighten the gulls. She didn't bother to close the slider. Stubby finished his meal and flew off. Unable to put weight on either leg, Stumpy was still struggling to stay upright, let alone eat. That would make Fran's job easier. Holding out the sausage and making calming noises, she slowly advanced toward the bird.

"Here's something for you, sweetie." She squatted down and held out the treat.

Used to taking food from her, Stumpy didn't hesitate. As he snatched the offering from her fingers, she grabbed him.

The bird squawked and tried to flap his wings. "It's okay," she soothed.

Taking care not to hold him too tightly, she glanced at Mitch, who had abandoned his breakfast and stood ready to help. "Mitch? Will you check to make sure the cage door is open and bring it outside?"

"You want it on the patio table?"

"Yes, please."

Once the open cage was ready, Fran carefully set the agitated bird inside. She latched the door, then covered the cage with the blanket. Instantly, Stumpy stopped squawking.

"See how the darkness calms him? That and the tranquilizer. I'll be back, Stumpy."

She dashed inside to grab her purse. Moments later, car keys in hand, she reached for the cage.

"How do you expect to carry that thing down all

those stairs?" Mitch nodded at the dozen steps leading from the deck to the ground. "I'll carry it. And you can put those keys away. We'll take my car."

Grateful as she was for his offer to help, she didn't want to interfere with his work. "What about your book?"

"This won't take long, will it? The work will keep."

THE VET'S OFFICE was on the outskirts of town. Mitch drove while Fran sat in the backseat beside the blanket-draped cage and called out driving directions. Between telling him where to turn she spoke to the bird in a soft, cooing voice Mitch never had heard.

No one had ever fussed over *him* this way. As a kid, when he was sick, his mother had read to him until he'd been old enough to read himself. Then she'd bought him books but had pretty much left him alone. After her death, his father had all but ignored him when he was sick, to "make you tough." With Fran fussing over him, catching the flu wouldn't be half bad.

But she wasn't going to fuss over him. She wouldn't even kiss him again.

By the time he pulled into the semicrowded parking lot of a one-story, wood building, it looked like rain. He parked as close to the door as possible.

He offered to carry the cage, but Fran shook her head. "He'll be calmer if I stay close," she said, hugging the bulky thing as she hurried toward the door.

Mitch's parents hadn't liked animals, and he'd never been to a vet's office. The place smelled of disinfectant and animal. Still holding the cage, Fran checked in at the front desk with a gawky, college-aged boy, whose name tag identified him as Thad. Obviously, she'd been here before. As she and Thad exchanged greetings and talked about some *Animal Planet* show they both watched, Mitch noted his red face and awed expression. Kid had a major crush on her. Well, he had good taste.

Standing at her shoulder, Mitch caught a whiff of her hair, which smelled clean and sweet. It reminded him of last night and how she'd kissed him with heat and passion.

He leaned closer to her warmth, caught himself and frowned, then backed away and checked out the small waiting room adjacent to the check-in desk. Three women, one man and their leashed, woofing dogs and caged, meowing cats, sat on chairs, thumbing through magazines and waiting.

Once Stumpy joined the group there was sure to be plenty more racket. No fan of noise, Mitch dreaded that.

"Dr. Tess says to go right in," Thad said, to Mitch's relief.

Fran turned to him. "If you'd rather wait here—"

Not about to miss any of the fun, Mitch shook his head. He followed Fran down a short hall to the first room.

She set the cage on a steel exam table, then rearranged the blanket over it. Mitch stood on the other side. Her face was pale with worry. He wished he could comfort her in some small way, but didn't know how.

"I'm sure he'll be okay," he said gruffly.

"Of course he will." Her lips curled but her eyes were filled with doubt.

Seconds later, the door opened and the middle-aged vet strode in, buttoning her white lab coat. She gave a friendly smile. "Good to see you, Fran. I'll be rooting for you at the cook-off."

"Thank you." Fran glanced at Mitch. "This is Mitch, my…friend. Meet Dr. Tess Martin."

"Dr. Tess is fine."

"Pleasure, Dr. Tess," he said, shaking her hand.

Moving out of her way, he joined Fran.

"I understand you've brought Stumpy, not Stubby, this time."

Fran nodded. "Silly bird injured his good leg."

"Let's take a look." Dr. Tess snapped on latex gloves. "Shall I take him out of his cage?"

"I will," Fran said. "I fed him one of those tranquilizer tablets you gave me, so it shouldn't be too hard."

Somber, she removed the blanket, then pulled the gull, who seemed calm, from the cage.

As Dr. Tess gently examined the leg, Mitch followed his instincts and put his arm around Fran's shoulders. She shot him a grateful look that made him feel good.

"It looks broken," the vet said. "How'd you do that, Stumpy?"

"Will he be all right?" Fran asked, biting her lip.

Tess shook her head. "Not with the other leg useless. In my opinion it would be best to euthanize him."

Mitch squeezed her shoulder in sympathy. But Fran pulled away and shook her head. "Put him down? Stumpy doesn't want to die." Her mouth tightened. "That is not an option."

He caught the vet's eye and shrugged.

"I could put a splint on the leg until it heals," she said at last. "But that means you'll have to feed and water him twice a day and watch him carefully. You'll want to pick up some vitamins from the Wild Bird Store to supplement his diet. Keep him outside in a sheltered area and in the cage to protect him from predators and give him an old towel or a scrap of blanket to keep warm."

"I can do that."

"There is one more thing. He's used to flying free. Being trapped in a cage could kill him."

"It won't," Fran said in a firm voice. "I'll take good care of him until he's healed and ready to be on his own again."

That she was willing to spend money and time caring for a wild bird amazed Mitch, but also made sense. She could no more let this creature die than she could close the Oceanside and move away. He admired and liked her more than ever.

"All right," Dr. Tess said. "I'll give him a dose of antibiotics to ward off infection. Then I'll tape his leg. If he survives, bring him back in two weeks." She gave her head a grave shake. "But I'm afraid you're setting yourself up for heartache."

HUNKERED BEFORE the cage Mitch had placed under the eaves, Fran slid a water bowl inside Stumpy's cage. He seemed content. That could be due to the sedative or the blanket he was burrowed into. Or maybe the soft rain beyond the shelter of the deck comforted him.

"How's the patient doing?" Mitch asked, rolling down his sleeves.

Instead of going upstairs to work, he'd cleaned up the breakfast dishes—his way of helping out, she supposed. She appreciated that he'd come with her earlier and that he was here now.

"As well as can be expected." She stood and turned to him. "Thanks for being here."

"No problem." The warmth in his smile matched his eyes. "Stumpy's lucky to have you."

Fran hoped so. The truth was, she was worried. She chafed her arms, then shivered. "Do you think he'll survive?"

"Hey." Mitch pulled her into a hug. "If anybody can save him, you can."

She wasn't used to being comforted—she usually reassured others. Savoring the moment and the heaven of Mitch's arms around her, she closed her eyes and burrowed close against his solid warmth.

His hold tightened. He kissed the top of her head. Then her temple. Her heart began to thud. Heat pulsed through her and suddenly comfort was the last thing on her mind. She wanted this man.

Unable to stop herself, she lifted her face.

"Fran," he murmured in a voice laced with need.

As he lowered his head, the gull squawked. They backed away from each other.

"Sorry about that," he said.

Fran nodded and silently thanked the gull. For a moment there, she'd forgotten that she shouldn't kiss Mitch. He seemed to have forgotten, too.

"What's the matter, Stumpy?" she asked, moving to the cage.

The bird blinked and ignored her.

"Maybe he thinks we should get a room," Mitch quipped. But his face was dead-serious.

Considering that anyone could walk onto the deck at

any time and catch her passionately kissing Mitch—her guest!—that made good sense.

What made no sense was that she'd been ready to do just that—give herself to him without a care about the consequences. If not for the gull…

She needed to leave, right now, and get hold of herself.

"Maybe he wants some alone time," she said as light as you please. She headed for the slider. "I know I do. I really should run those errands now."

"And I should work." Mitch raked his hand through his hair. At a distance, he followed her inside. "I'll see you later."

Chapter Eight

Restless and burning, Mitch headed upstairs to work, which was a joke, since, at the moment, he was so damned frustrated he doubted he'd do much of anything. Then again, last night had been just as bad, yet he'd managed to sketch out part of a full chapter. It didn't have much depth, he'd have to flesh it out, but it was something.

He'd felt so damned good earlier. The gratitude in Fran's eyes at the vet's and the closeness they'd shared bringing the gull home. But now…

He wanted her more than ever. She wanted him, too. Every time she looked his way, he saw the desire in her eyes. Nothing stood between them except Fran herself.

Mitch respected that she didn't want a short-term relationship. That didn't change how he felt.

He sat down at the desk and woke up the computer, his thoughts returning to the busy morning. Fran's insistence on working to save Stumpy. Mitch shook his head. He'd never met a woman like her. She was special—passionate, thoughtful and considerate, a one-of-a-kind woman who deserved a man capable of loving and cherishing her forever.

Mitch wished he was like that, because the thought of her with some other man was unthinkable. He bypassed the manuscript to scan his e-mail. Another from his agent, labeled Urgent. More from his publicist and his editor. All three had left voice mails on his cell phone, but he hadn't listened to them. Didn't want to deal with the pressure or their questions.

Screw e-mail. He thought about a visit to Foster's, but it was pouring and he needed to work. Unfortunately, his mind refused to cooperate and his thoughts returned to Fran. He fantasized about taking her hair down and kissing her everywhere, making her pant with need. Then, when she could stand it no more, he'd… His body stirred and he could not focus.

Well, hell. His stomach rumbled. It was way past lunchtime. Shoving his hands into his jeans pockets he wandered downstairs. Fran still was out, and he should check on the damned bird. Standing under the eaves he peered at Stumpy, who sat unmoving and appeared to be looking out at the ocean. Mitch couldn't tell if he was unhappy or not.

"You'd better not die," he warned.

Stumpy opened his beak, then closed it. Mitch figured that was a good sign. Maybe he was hungry, too. "I'll be back with food," he said.

He was in the kitchen, rummaging through the refrigerator for the gull's lunch, when the garage door hummed open. Fran was back.

Her footsteps sounded on the basement steps.

Slightly breathless, she entered the kitchen with two bulging grocery bags.

"Mitch." Surprise colored her face. "I didn't expect to see you."

"Taking a break."

He took the bags from her and set them on the counter. Her skin was pink from the wind and a chin-length lock of hair that had escaped her braid looked wet. "You got rained on."

"Boy, did I. In the grocery parking lot."

Unable to restrain himself, he tucked the lock behind her ear, his hand lingering there to trace the delicate shell of her ear.

Her eyes darkened, beckoning him closer. But she said she didn't want that. He dropped his hand and stepped back.

"H-how's Stumpy?" she asked, dropping her purse onto a chair.

"Calm and dry, but hungry, I think. I was looking for something to feed him."

"Then, even if I did get wet, it's a good thing I stopped at the grocery."

The desire on her face played havoc with his will-power.

"I'm hungry, too," he growled, hardly aware of his words.

"You haven't eaten yet?" Fran darted a glance at the clock. "It's long past lunchtime."

"Not for food. For you." Swearing softly, he curled his hands into fists. "The way you're looking at me… it's damned dangerous. You shouldn't do that to a man unless you want him to love you."

She swallowed. Shot him a pleading look that either meant, kiss me or you misunderstood.

"Mitch, I can't—"

Suddenly, the phone rang.

"I'll get that." Fran spun away.

Needing to know what she'd been about to say, he clasped her wrist. "Forget the phone and talk to me."

She turned toward him. Bit her lip. The machine picked up. It was one of those answering machines where the caller's message was easy to hear.

"Mitch, it's Kathryn. I can't reach you on your cell and you don't answer your e-mail, so I'm hoping you'll get this message. Sylvia's worried about you, and so am I. Jakes is getting antsy, and I can't put him off much longer. Call me right away."

Desire forgotten, Mitch swore.

"Who are Kathryn and those other people?" Fran asked with slightly widened eyes.

He scrubbed his hand over his face. "Kathryn Shuster is my agent, Sylvia Patterson is my publicist. Peter Jakes is my editor."

He waited for more questions, but Fran had the grace to keep her mouth shut. Yet, he could see by her curious expression that she was dying to know more. This was nobody's business but his.

"You want to know why they're worried?" he blurted out. "Because I can't write this friggin' book."

Admitting it out loud shamed him. He was frustrated and furious with himself, and he lashed out at her. "Too damned many distractions." He glanced at her breasts, her mouth, then glared at her stunned face. "I came here to be alone, and all I can think about is you. Let me be!"

She reeled as if he'd slapped her. Scum that he was, he wheeled away and strode out.

ROSY'S DINER was packed, as usual. As hungry customers and bustling waitresses filled the restaurant with noise, Fran laid her napkin beside her half-empty plate. "What did you say?"

This Wednesday night meeting, one of the many before the Cranberry Festival, had started a good forty-five minutes ago, and she was having trouble keeping her mind on the conversation.

Anne Trueblood, an attorney and volunteer across the table, shot her a puzzled look. "That we have thirty entrants for the pie eating contest," she said in a voice that easily competed with the clamor.

"That's great," Fran said without much enthusiasm.

"No, it isn't," Anne said. "Last year we had twelve. We all just agreed that we don't have the space for thirty. What's with you tonight, Fran?"

At the head of the table, Cammie Blanco, the attractive, blonde events planner in charge of the volunteers, eyed her. "You do seem preoccupied. Are you feeling all right?"

No. She felt bruised and mad. She'd started out wanting to give Mitch peace and quiet. Then he'd claimed she inspired him and kissed her. Now he blamed her for his problems. The dark look on his face while he listened to the message, and the anger that followed... Fran hated that, but thank God for the timing. That call had saved her from sharing her feelings and making a huge mistake.

As for his hurtful words, this time he'd gone too far.

She hadn't decided what she'd do about it and didn't want to think about Mitch.

"Just thinking about the cook-off," she said.

"You nervous?" asked John Pearson, a retiree from the cranberry factory. He also was a contestant.

"Not at all. Are you?"

"How can I be when I'm gonna win?"

His teasing smile made her feel better.

"What are you cooking?" Mike Rufous, a contractor, asked them both.

"That's proprietary information," John said.

Fran nodded.

Rosy, the fiftysomething owner of Rosy's, appeared with a coffeepot. "Mitch Matthews was in here the other night. He sure is something."

She *would* mention Mitch. The other women at the table murmured agreement—except for Cammie, who recently had married photographer Curt Blanco in the Oceanside great room.

"He is good-looking." She smiled. "But not quite as handsome as Curt."

Rosy laughed before focusing again on Fran. "How does it feel, sharing your B and B with Mitch and nobody else?"

The entire group, Rosy included, cast speculative glances Fran's way. The nosy woman ferreted out everything about everyone, then freely shared the information. Well, she'd get nothing tonight.

"He's busy with a project, so I don't see much of him," Fran replied in a casual tone.

And there was her answer for what to do. She'd go back to her original plan of cooking breakfast, period.

No more sitting with him while he ate or anything beyond the courtesies all her guests received. Polite but distant, that was her new motto. Starting this instant, Mitch Matthews was out of her system. He was.

Looking disappointed, Rosy shook her head. She opened her mouth to say God knew what.

Fran spoke first. "Wait til you hear what happened to Stumpy."

Busy with the posters and last-minute details for the Cranberry Festival, she hadn't yet shared the news. Now she filled in Rosy and everyone else at the table. "He'll be stuck in a cage for two weeks. Then we go back to Dr. Tess for a checkup."

"Poor thing," Rosy said.

Subject neatly changed. Fran heaved a silent sigh of relief.

"With you taking care of him, he'll be fine in no time," Anne said.

Mitch had voiced the same sentiment. Fran hoped they were right.

As Rosy offered coffee, she covered her cup and shook her head. "Speaking of Stumpy, I should go home and check on him." She glanced at Cammie. "If we're through here?"

Cammie glanced at her watch, then nodded. "I should get home to Curt, too. Thanks for the hard work, everyone. See you all next week. Only two more meetings before the festival."

Two-plus weeks before the cook-off, and Fran hadn't even attempted to bake today. Any more of that and she'd lose for sure.

From now on, she'd divide the bulk of her attention

between Stumpy, perfecting the recipe and getting ready for the baby shower Saturday night. As for Mitch's breakfast, that was last on the list.

If he didn't like that he could just…check out early. She was too angry to even feel sad at the thought. And far too busy to waste more time thinking about him.

WALKING THE BEACH at night was cold business. Hunching his shoulders against the fine mist Mitch aimed the flashlight taken from the glove compartment of his car at the sand. Moving quickly, he rounded the curve in the beach. Minutes later he stepped onto Foster's porch, wiped his feet on the mat and knocked.

Inside, he heard the thud of footsteps. Then the porch light flashed on and the door swung open. Foster's eyes widened, probably because Mitch hadn't been here in days, and never at night.

"Mitch." He stepped back. "Come in."

"There's a baby shower at the Oceanside tonight," Mitch said by way of explaining.

So what if his suite was three flights up and insulated from the noise. He'd bought earplugs, too. But he'd know they were downstairs. Besides, he felt like hell.

"It's chilly outside," Foster said.

"You're telling me."

Foster had built a fire in the stove in the corner, and the pleasant smell of burning wood filled the place. Mitch hung his jacket over Foster's on the back of the door, then moved in front of the stove and stretched out his hands. The heat felt good.

"Want a cup of tea, or a snort? There's a bottle of scotch in the kitchen cabinet."

"No, thanks."

Returning to the sofa—Mitch had never seen Foster sit anyplace but his work chair—Foster glanced at the open book he'd obviously been reading. *The Essays of Bertrand Russell*. Weighty stuff.

"Don't let me interrupt you," Mitch said. He wasn't ready to leave the warmth of the fire.

For once, Foster didn't speak, just nodded and returned to the book.

The room filled with comfortable silence. So different from the chill inside the Oceanside, which was Mitch's doing. Since he'd yelled at Fran Wednesday, she'd turned remote and cool, giving him all the space a man could want.

He'd tried to apologize, but having acted like a jerk one too many times, she'd brushed him off. That she might not forgive him was tearing him apart. Wretched, he released a heavy sigh and scrubbed the back of his neck.

"Sit down, son."

Foster gestured at the other end of the worn sofa. Apparently, he didn't want Mitch sitting in his work chair. Or dragging in a chair from the kitchen.

Mitch ambled over and sat.

"You're not really a tourist, are you?"

"Not this year. I came here to work. I'm writing a book."

And that statement was the lie of the year. He hadn't written a single word since Tuesday. Even so, he'd contacted Kathryn and Sylvia, promising that the manuscript would be done on time. Kathryn had pacified Peter Jakes, and Sylvia no longer worried that she'd have to cancel his two-week signing tour. Now to live up to his commitment…

"You're a wanderer." Foster stroked his chin. "And you don't know where you're headed."

Mitch grimaced. "What are you, psychic?"

"Just a keen observer. All artists are." After a few moments of silence, Foster fixed him with a kindly, but intent stare. "There's a reason you wandered to Cranberry and specifically the Oceanside, and her name is Fran. What happened? Did you two have words?"

The damned man really was perceptive. Mitch hung his head and nodded. "The writing isn't going well, and I took it out on her. I said things…" Remembering, he cringed. "I really screwed up."

"Did you apologize?"

"Yeah, but she's still mad."

"Do it again, and she'll be all right."

"You think?"

"If you really mean it."

He would. He wished he could talk to her tonight, but not with the baby shower. After, she'd be tired.

"I'll do it first thing in the morning," he said.

Foster scratched his earlobe, then stayed quiet awhile. Finally, he eyed Mitch. "There's something else you're sadly lacking. Balance."

Not sure he'd heard right, Mitch frowned. "Balance?"

"All work and no play? You know the saying."

Mitch had often reminded others to balance their lives, but never had applied the advice to himself. Talk about the shoemaker needing new shoes…

Snickering, he shook his head. "You're right." He

glanced at Foster's tools, spread across the TV table by his work chair. "I think I'm ready for that carving lesson."

BY TEN-THIRTY Saturday night most of the people who had gathered in the great room for Cinnamon and Nick's baby shower had gone. Only Cinnamon and Nick, his sister, Sharon, her almost fifteen-year-old daughter, Abby, and Sharon's boyfriend, Andy, remained. They sat around the massive stone fireplace, talking quietly and enjoying the hiss and pop of the cedar logs—Fran's first fire of the season.

Comfortably sprawled in one of the pair of arm-chairs, Fran yawned.

Cinnamon, who was seated beside Nick on the love seat, elbowed her husband. "Fran's tired. We should go."

In no hurry for them to leave, Fran sat up straight. "Please, stay a while longer. I'm enjoying this."

A nice change from the awful tension whenever Mitch was here. He'd gone out, but what would happen if he walked in now? Would her guests sense the strain between them?

At the moment, Fran felt too mellow to worry about that. "Would anyone like more coffee or tea, or food? There are a few of Alice Caroline's chocolates left."

"No, thanks."

"I've had enough."

"I couldn't," Nick replied, then glanced at his wife. "How about you, babe?"

Making a face, Cinnamon rubbed her enormous belly. "I couldn't eat another thing." Her mouth quirked. "But I'd love to take home those extra chocolates."

This was quite a change from two weeks ago, when she was always hungry. But then, plenty had changed. She'd grown even bigger. And Fran had followed her plan, treating Mitch civilly but just barely. Holding herself aloof, especially toward Mitch, was counter to her nature, but the situation demanded distance.

To Mitch's credit, he'd tried to apologize. But Fran wasn't ready to let him off so easily, not this time. Now they spoke only when necessary, usually at breakfast, which she served, then disappeared until he finished. He was bathed in the quiet and solitude he wanted.

They were like strangers and if that hurt, eventually she'd get over it.

"So many wonderful things for the baby." Cinnamon gestured at the pile of gifts spread over the coffee table and floor. She smiled at Fran. "Thanks for a shower I'll never forget. You're the best friend ever."

"You're very welcome," Fran said.

With his arm around his wife, Nick glanced at Fran. "Never thought I'd say this, but I enjoyed myself. This was a lot more fun than the shower they gave Cinnamon at work."

"Sure was," said Andy, who shared the sofa with Sharon.

They both worked at the cranberry factory and had dated for close to three years. That he'd come with her to a party most men avoided at all costs showed how much he cared for her.

Abby, who sat cross-legged on the area rug, nodded. "I've never been to a baby shower. This was really fun." She picked up a tiny striped sleeper, her face filled with wonder. "Will a baby really fit into this?"

"When you were born you were that little," Sharon said.

"I was? I can't wait to meet my cousin."

"You won't have to wait much longer," Fran said. "November fifteenth is what, six weeks from now?"

A math whiz slated for college scholarships and a stellar future, Abby glanced thoughtfully upward. "Actually it's forty days—if you don't count today."

"Unless Cassie decides to show up early." Nick placed his palm over the baby. "You really ought to stop working now, babe. The factory will survive without you."

Cinnamon rolled her eyes. "Don't you remember what Dr. Bartlett said at our last two appointments? We're right on time. If I stop working now I'll just sit around, waiting. That'd drive both of us crazy." She folded her arms. "I intend to work right up until I deliver."

"You're the boss, Mama." Nick gave her a teasing grin.

In companionable silence Fran and her friends watched the dying fire. After a while, Andy and Sharon exchanged looks, then Sharon gave a fractional nod.

"Sharon and I have exciting news." He clasped her hand. "We're getting married."

"Andy's going to be my stepdad?" Abby crowed. "Wahoo!"

"Isn't it wonderful?" Sharon's eyes shone. "Now I can wear my ring." Andy slid the diamond from his jeans pocket and pushed it onto Sharon's ring finger.

Cinnamon lumbered up, and the rest of the group stood and gathered round to admire it.

"It's beautiful," Fran said. "Congratulations. I'm thrilled for you." Envious, too.

"I always hoped for this day." Beaming, Cinnamon hugged them both.

When she let them go, Nick hugged his sister and shook hands with Andy. "Welcome to the family."

"I think I'll sit down again." Resisting help, Cinnamon lowered herself to the sofa.

Everyone else followed suit.

"This calls for a toast," Nick said. "Got any champagne, Fran?"

She nodded. "I'll open a bottle, and sparkling cider for you, Cinnamon."

"Do I get champagne, too?" Abby looked hopeful.

"Not for a few years yet," Sharon said.

"Rats."

"You like sparkling cider," Fran reminded her. "You can help me in the kitchen, too. First, though, I want to know why Andy and your mom didn't say anything at the shower. We all could have toasted you."

"We didn't want to steal Cinnamon and Nick's thunder," Sharon said. "Besides, we're eating at Rosy's tomorrow night. I don't plan on taking off this ring ever again. She'll see it, and that'll take care of spreading the news."

Knowing laughter filled the room.

Five minutes later, Fran and Abby brought in a tray of glasses, the champagne and juice. While they poured the drinks, Andy looked at Fran.

"Sharon and I want to have the ceremony right here, in the great room."

"I would love that. We haven't had a wedding here since Cammie and Curt got married last year."

Weddings were such fun, joyful events. Fran wished

she could experience the happiness firsthand, but, at the rate she was going, that didn't seem likely. Like her aunt Frannie, she seemed destined to forever play hostess, never the bride. A disheartening thought, but now was no time to feel sorry for herself.

She forced a smile. "Do you have a date in mind?"

"We're thinking mid-March, after the Valentine's Day rush and before tourist season heats up."

"Perfect."

Fran glanced at the two couples, their deep love for each other obvious. That was what she wanted, true love and forever after. Not lopsided, unrequited feelings for a man who wasn't built for love. "Shall we toast?"

When all glasses were raised, she said what was in her heart. "May your marriage be long and your lives be filled with bliss."

Silently she added, *And may I find what you have.*

Chapter Nine

Though Mitch had enjoyed his first wood-carving lesson and had returned to the Oceanside hopeful of getting back into Fran's good graces in the morning, he'd spent a restless night, his sleep broken by a repeating nightmare. He was stranded alone on an island with no way to get back and nothing but his latest manuscript to keep him company. The sun faded the ink and soon the pages were blank.

A ridiculous dream, yet he was badly shaken. What would Foster make of it? No doubt he'd have good insights, but Mitch wasn't about to share. What he needed was what he'd missed most lately—Fran's warmth and friendly conversation.

Despite the invisible mountain between them, Mitch aimed to take Foster's advice and apologize with total sincerity.

He started slowly, with a smile. "'Morning."

Fran did not return the smile. "Good morning," she said with a stiff nod.

Despite the comfortable temperature of the room, Mitch felt cold. He poured coffee for himself.

"How was the baby shower?" By the time he'd come home everyone was gone and Fran had disappeared into her basement apartment.

"Lots of fun."

She turned away to take something from the oven. Wishing he could see her face, he sat down. As she delivered a cheese omelet and two slabs of fried ham, he tried again.

"You built a fire last night." He'd smelled the burning wood and had noticed the glowing embers. "I'll bet your guests enjoyed that."

She nodded.

"How's Stumpy this morning?"

"Recovering well. On Wednesday—" Abruptly she cut herself off, grabbed the coffee and topped off his mug.

"You'll what?" he coaxed, spearing a steaming forkful of his omelet. As always, it tasted delicious.

"Take him back to Dr. Tess. Hopefully, she'll take off the splint and give the go-ahead to set him free."

"If you want me to come with…" he offered, shrugging.

"No, thank you."

If she showed him that wooden smile one more time, he'd lose it. Time for that apology.

He set down his fork. "I can't stand this anymore."

"Stand what?" she asked, retreating again into the kitchen.

"This awkwardness between us. I tried to apologize and you wouldn't listen. What do you want me to do?"

"Sound like you're really sorry, for starters." She pulled her braid over her shoulder and fiddled with the hair tie on the end, then let go and fixed him with a dirty look. "A glib, 'I'm sorry' isn't enough."

Foster had been right. Mitch bowed his head, then looked at her. "I truly am sorry for what I said."

Her expression changed a hair, giving him hope.

He met her gaze straight on, letting her see that he was sincere. "You deserve better."

Her body language—head angled and arms crossed—told him she needed more.

"My writing troubles have nothing to do with you," he said. "I shouldn't have blamed or attacked you. You didn't try to distract me, I did that to myself. I'm the one who pursued you and kissed you." She'd kissed him back, but he wasn't stupid. He left out that fact. "Now you're freezing me out, and I'm miserable. I miss you."

"I appreciate your saying so." Her eyes softened. "I accept your apology."

As sweet as that felt, Mitch needed to say more. At the very least, he owed her an honest explanation, pathetic as it might make him look.

"The truth is, I haven't been able to write since my father died," he said. Difficult as it was to lay his weakness bare, he refused to flinch from her gaze. "I thought if I changed the scenery and came here, I'd get back on track. What I said about you? I meant that. You inspire me more than you'll ever know. But you and the change of scenery aren't enough."

"Mitch—"

Needing to finish his thought, he held up his hand, silencing her. "Foster Gravis says I need balance in my life, something to do besides work. As valid as that

point is, it doesn't excuse my actions." Unable to bear
her pity for the next part, he ducked his head. "I've lost
my creativity."

Stating the awful truth to her was like confessing his
sins. He prayed for her absolution.

"I'm glad you and Foster are friends," she said, leaning against the refrigerator. "But I'm thinking that
maybe you need to mourn your father's passing before
you can be creative again."

There wasn't a trace of censure in her voice, only
warmth. The icy knot in Mitch's chest began to loosen
and thaw. He raised his head and the tenderness and affection he saw in Fran's face touched him—he would
cling to them like a lifeline.

"I told you my parents died," she continued. "That
was twelve years ago. The year that followed is a
complete blur for me. I was an automaton, going
through the motions of life without really being
present."

She hesitated. "Something else sad happened. You
know I was engaged once. That was eight years ago."
Her gaze dropped to a smudge on her apron before she
finished in a low voice. "I was also expecting a baby.
When I was ten weeks along, I miscarried. Not long
after, Leif broke off our engagement and walked out."
She bit her lip. "Turned out, he only wanted to get married because of the baby. That's when I moved into the
Oceanside with Aunt Frannie. A year after that, I lost
her, too."

Leif sounded like a cruel bastard. Mitch swore. Losing a baby and its father, with no parents to help you
through, then losing your aunt… So much loss. He

couldn't imagine. He truly admired Fran's strength and ability to enjoy life after all this hardship.

"If I could, I'd rearrange the bastard's face."

"I appreciate that," she said with a wry smile. "My point is, loss is painful and surviving can be a real struggle. But eventually I got through it. And so will you."

She believed in him—he saw it in her eyes.

Emotion rose in his chest and clogged his throat. He swallowed thickly. "Were you close to your parents?"

"Pretty much."

"My father and I weren't close until a few weeks before he died."

"But the connection was there, all the same. That's why you can't write, Mitch. You're grieving."

His father would've had a different word for it— weak. "I'm not like you, Fran. I don't need a year. It's been over eight months, time I moved on."

"Sorry, but there's no timetable on the grieving process."

Whether she was right or wrong, he was profoundly grateful that they were talking again. "There ought to be," he said gruffly.

"Is there anything I can do to help?"

"Hope for a miracle."

"Anything else?"

Sincerity rang in her voice and shone from her face, so he said what was in his heart. "Don't ever do that again."

"Do what?"

"Freeze me out."

"Then don't blame me for your problems."

"Fair enough."

BY LATE TUESDAY Mitch had written sixteen pages. Not high-quality stuff, but progress, all the same. Amazing.

How and why, he didn't know, but he suspected that making up with Fran at breakfast Sunday had something to do with the breakthrough. That and the two wood-carving lessons from Foster, for which he paid. Otherwise, he'd told Foster, there would be no lessons.

Despite Mitch's clumsiness, wood carving was surprisingly enjoyable. It calmed his mind and refreshed his spirit. In time, he might even show Fran the results. For now, he kept his new endeavor to himself.

He did share his writing progress with her at breakfast Wednesday morning.

"Sixteen pages—that's wonderful!" As she ladled steaming oatmeal into a bowl she flashed a smile that dazzled him.

He grinned back. "Nothing like having my own private cheerleader."

"Rah, rah ram, you the man." Laughing, she set the bowl in front of him, along with a sizzling plate of bacon.

He caught a whiff of vanilla and woman. Fierce desire sucker-punched him, and it was all he could do not to pull her onto his lap. But he wasn't going there, not after finally righting things between them. He gripped the napkin in his fist.

"What's the matter, Mitch?" she said, frowning.

"You smell good."

"I do? Thank you."

Her eyes lit with pleasure. Big, liquid eyes a man could get lost in. For a moment, against his better judgment, Mitch did.

Fran flushed. Tearing his gaze away he added brown

sugar and milk to his oatmeal. She nodded toward the slider. "There's Stubby, waiting for breakfast beside Stumpy's cage. After two weeks they still eat together. Isn't that dear?"

What was sweet was Fran's tender expression. "I don't see any oatmeal out there."

"They don't like it. They get scrambled eggs with their bacon. Stumpy's last caged meal."

She piled their plates with food. As he had every day, even when she was mad at him, Mitch opened the slider for her, closed it behind her—the air was biting and damp—and returned to his breakfast. The oatmeal was delicious, but, with his attention on Fran, he barely tasted it. She set Stubby's plate on the deck, then opened the door of the cage and slipped Stumpy's plate inside.

She stood back with her hands at her sides, watching both gulls with an adoring smile that made Mitch's chest hurt. If the gulls didn't feel like a million bucks they were sorry excuses for birds.

"I'm coming with you to the vet's," he said as Fran reentered the room.

"You can't spare the time. I'll manage by myself."

She was right about the time, but going with her seemed important. "I don't mind the break, and you shouldn't drive with the bird to look after. Besides, I want to be there to see Dr. Tess's face when she sees how fat and sassy Stumpy is."

"In that case, as soon as you finish eating, we'll go."

Half an hour later, he stood beside Fran in the same exam room as before while Dr. Tess examined the sedated bird.

After removing the splint and examining the leg, she smiled. "The leg is healed. Stumpy looks great."

"And you wanted to euthanize him," Mitch said, unable to help himself.

Fran shot him a don't-rub-it-in frown, but he figured the vet could handle it.

"I never thought he'd survive," Dr. Tess said. "Happily, I was wrong. You're a miracle worker, Fran. How'd you do it?"

"I talked to him and made sure he had enough to eat and drink and that he was protected from the rain. And his buddy, Stubby, kept him company."

"Gulls mate for life, you know," Dr. Tess said. "My guess is, Stubby is his mate."

"Stubby's a girl? Hmm." Fran looked thoughtful. "Maybe I should change her name to Stubette."

"Or Mrs. Stumpy," Mitch quipped. "The 'gullfriend' may have helped Stumpy's morale, but Fran did the tough stuff. She loved him back to health."

His words earned him a smile.

"I treated him the same way I treat my guests."

When they didn't act like a jerk.

"No wonder the Oceanside is so popular," Dr. Tess said. "After the sedative wears off in an hour or so, you can release him."

"Did you hear that, Stumpy? You'll soon be free again."

Mitch loaded Stumpy's cage into the backseat of his car, and Fran sat in front.

"We should do something to celebrate Stumpy's recovery," he said as he pulled into the driveway. The second the words were out he wanted to call them back. A celebration with Fran could be dangerous.

To his relief she shook her head. "His flying off is enough for me. We definitely should watch that. Then you have to write that book, and I should work on my recipe. The cook-off is only ten days away, and I'm not ready. And there's still so much to do before the festival—meetings and crazy, last-minute details. No time for celebrations."

She sounded stressed. "It'll all get done," he assured her.

"Only if I work hard."

A not-so-subtle message that applied to him, as well. He intended to do just that.

As he pulled to a stop to the side of the garage, she glanced at him. "I still need a name for those cranberry bars. Have you thought of anything?"

He'd forgotten about that. "Not yet, but I will."

As FRAN STOOD on the deck beside the blanket-covered cage, the brisk wind whipped her cords against her legs and slapped her cheeks. She pointed at the gull circling over the beach. "Look, Mitch, I think that's Stubby. She knows we're about to set Stumpy free."

"Seems that way." His face was red with cold and his hair tossed and wild.

He seemed genuinely pleased for the gull. Fran felt blessed to have his support and friendship and relieved that they'd patched up their differences.

Squinting against the wind, he smiled at her. She saw the affection there and her heart felt full to overflowing. With amazement she realized that, at some point, she'd moved beyond caring for Mitch to a deeper place. She loved him. A few weeks from now when he left, she'd end up hurt, but, at the moment, she was too awash in the sweetness of it to care.

"It's time," she said, moving to the cage. "Are you ready, Stumpy?" She pulled the blanket from it.

The bird flapped his wings, opened his beak and screeched his gull cry.

"The sedative has worn off," she told Mitch.

He plugged his ears. "So I hear."

She laughed. "He'll stop soon. You're about to fly free," she said, speaking softly to calm him.

She unlatched the door, then stood back. Mitch put his arm around her shoulders as if it were the most natural thing in the world. Relaxed and happy, her attention on Stumpy, Fran sank against him.

For a moment, the gull simply blinked. Then he shot through the door. Together Fran and Mitch watched him soar over the ocean, his mate at his side.

"Goodbye, Stumpy." Fran sniffled. "Don't forget to come back for breakfast tomorrow."

Mitch glanced at her with surprise. "Don't tell me you're sad about this."

She shook her head. "They're together, and I'm thrilled for them both."

"You're a romantic."

"Hopeless."

"How is it I never realized?"

"Guess you're not such an expert on people, after all," she said, smiling so he'd know she was teasing.

"So I've learned. But you and Foster are teaching me."

His arm stayed around her as they headed for the slider. She ought to bring in the blanket and cage, but, at the moment, she was too content.

Once inside, Mitch let go of her, then helped her out of her coat, his hand grazing her shoulder. Her nerves began to thrum and suddenly the very air seemed charged and potent, as if lightning were about to strike.

The love in her chest made her want what she shouldn't, and she knew that soon she would kiss him again. Fully aware of the consequences of her actions she turned into him and slid her palms up his chest.

He trapped her wrists with his hands. "What are you doing?"

"Thanking you for coming to the vet's, then standing out there with me."

"Simple words are enough," he said, his gruff tone at odds with the hunger in his face.

"Not for something this momentous."

A muscle ticced in his jaw. She pulled one hand free and traced it.

Mitch stiffened. "You're playing with fire."

"Am I?" Urging his head down she kissed him.

FRAN'S ARMS were wrapped around Mitch's neck. She was doing hot things with her mouth, nibbling his bottom lip and making little sounds of pleasure.

Sometime between the trip to the vet's and letting Stumpy go, the emotions between them had shifted and intensified. Mitch didn't understand what had changed or why, only knew he shouldn't be kissing Fran. And now that she finally was in his arms, he couldn't let her go.

Her mouth parted and her tongue met his. His body sprang to life, and the hunger he'd corralled for days raged free, drowning out his control, his thoughts— everything but the warm, vital woman in his arms.

Long, deep kisses later, she was on the serving counter, her legs around his hips, the most sensitive part of her torturing his erection. He broke the kiss to nip her earlobe and tease the sensitive skin below it.

The moan he'd been waiting for without realizing it purled from her throat.

Blood roared through his head. Growling, he licked the hollow of her throat, unbuttoned her blouse, pulled it open and buried his face between her generous breasts. Her skin smelled of vanilla.

He cupped her breasts through her bra. The heavy roundness filled his hands and then some. *Sweet heaven.* His thumbs played over her taut nipples, making her gasp. They were both breathing hard now.

"How about we get rid of the bra?" he said, reaching behind her.

She nodded. He tugged it down and away. Her breasts spilled free, full and rosy-tipped. Better than any fantasy.

"You are luscious." He drank in the sight. Filled his hands and gently kneaded and teased.

More sounds of pleasure filled his ears like siren songs. He wanted to bury himself in her, make them both forget the world....

Get hold of yourself, warned a voice in his head.

What was he doing? He broke contact. Unwrapped her legs from his hips. "I didn't mean for things to go so far." Her bra and blouse lay haphazardly on the floor. Mitch retrieved both and handed them to her. "But I'm not sorry."

He looked at her kiss-swollen lips, flushed face and dazed expression. "I don't think you are, either."

Her fingers fumbled with her blouse, buttoning it

closed. Without the bra. Her nipples poked against the fabric. Mitch swallowed.

"I'm not." Fran glanced at his groin, her beautiful face flushed and alive. "I wanted this, too."

He burned to kiss her again and finish what they'd started. But that wasn't right. Fran wasn't a short-term affair kind of woman. She deserved more, things he couldn't give and promises he couldn't keep. In a few weeks, he'd be gone.

"See you at breakfast," he said.

Taking the stairs to the suite two at a time, he acknowledged that he'd already hurt her enough. The last thing he wanted was to cause her more pain. Between now and then, he'd keep his hands to himself.

Even if it killed him.

Chapter Ten

"Let me see that, Mitch." Foster turned the alderwood bowl Mitch had carved around in his hands. Alder was cheaper than oak or mahogany and, according to Foster, a good wood to learn on. "Not bad for a beginner. I had a hunch you'd be good at this."

To Mitch the lopsided bowl looked crude and rough, nowhere near as clean and finely honed as Foster's artistic creations. But he accepted the compliment.

Since the night of the baby shower, Foster had given him three lessons. Mitch had spent another few hours patiently shaping the bowl while Foster deftly created his birds and sea critters.

It was time Mitch should have spent at his computer, but he was glad to have learned the rudiments of woodworking.

"Monday I'll show you how to use the polisher I keep in the garage."

With only two weeks before he was supposed to finish the book and drive back to Seattle, Mitch was far behind where he should be. And starting to panic.

He shook his head. "Wish I could, but my deadline's

looming. From now on, it's work, work, work on the book. I doubt I'll even make it to the Cranberry Festival."

Except for the cook-off. He wasn't about to miss that.

"Leaving that bowl unfinished is a crying shame, but, if you can't, you can't."

They both stood and brushed wood chips from their clothes.

"Maybe if I drop by the day I leave—"

"I'll be working at the festival, then heading for Oklahoma for a week. My sister lives there, and neither of us is getting any younger."

Then this was the last time he'd see Foster. He'd miss this man, who'd become both friend and mentor. "I'd like to buy one of your pieces."

"So you said that first day we met. Which one calls to you?"

Mitch nodded at two gulls, beaks open and wings spread as if ready to take flight from their driftwood base. Foster had been working on it the first time Mitch had stopped by. "That one."

Foster stroked his chin and looked thoughtful. "Mind if I ask why?"

"The gulls reminded me of Stumpy and Stubby, the pair Fran feeds every morning. I thought I'd give it to her."

"She's still hot under the collar, huh?"

Mitch recalled the sizzling kisses they'd shared two days ago and their warm, lively breakfast conversations. She was hot, all right, but not the way Foster meant. He grinned. "Not after I took your advice and apologized the right way."

"Atta boy." Chuckling, the old man patted Mitch on

the back. "So you want to give Fran the gull carving because…"

"Because I know she'll love it. I'm thinking I'll give it to her right before I leave, as a thank-you for putting up with me."

The old man's eyes gleamed—he liked Mitch's reason. "Tell you what, you can have it, and no charge."

Mitch shook his head. "It's too valuable. I couldn't."

"You paid for your lessons and you let this old fella jabber at you for several weeks. That's payment enough. Take it." Foster pushed the wood carving into Mitch's arms.

"Thank you," Mitch said, overcome with his friend's generosity. "For the wood-carving lessons and everything else you taught me."

"It was a pleasure, son. Promise you won't give up the wood carving."

Balance. "I won't. I'm planning to pick up my own set of tools in Seattle."

"That's what I like to hear. Keep in touch and, next time you're in town, stop by."

EXACTLY ONE WEEK before the cook-off Fran cut into the latest attempt at the perfect cranberry bar, her sixth since she and Mitch had set Stumpy free. And shared kisses…and more. As wonderful as that had been and, despite the restless need in her body, she realized he'd been right to stop. And was grateful that he hadn't come near her since. Feeling as she did about him, making love would only worsen the pain of his leaving.

She bit into the bar. The perfect blend of flavors

burst on her tongue, with just the right texture—moist and chewy.

"Mmm," she murmured, closing her eyes to better savor the experience.

She opened them to find Mitch heading toward the kitchen, watching her with avid intensity. As if her eating a cranberry bar was sexy. Well, it *had* been a sensuous experience.

Not meant for his eyes, though. Since breakfast he'd been holed upstairs working—no beach walk today— and she hadn't expected to see him.

Self-conscious, she blotted her lips with a paper towel. "There you go, sneaking up on me again. How's the writing going?"

"So-so," he said, looking downcast. "That mouthwatering aroma is hard to resist, so I figured I'd take a break and beg a cranberry bar. Glad I did. Watching you is a treat. You even eat with passion, Fran. Was it as good as you made it look?"

Oh, what the heat in his gaze did to her. Flustered and aching with longing, she moved to the cabinet for a clean plate. "I'll let you judge for yourself." She cut him a generous chunk. "In my opinion this batch is perfect, but I would like a second opinion."

"Always game to help out there," he said, taking the plate to the kitchen table.

He looked good sitting there, as if he belonged. Her heart filled with love and she reminded herself that, a week from tomorrow, he'd drive away.

Refusing to think about that, she rested her hips against the kitchen sink, brushed off her apron and tried to look nonchalant. But, as he bit into the bar, she held her breath, watching his face. Mitch chewed and swallowed. He licked his lips and bit off more.

Unable to bear the suspense, she exhaled and leaned forward. "Well?"

"Fantastic," he said around a mouthful.

He'd never sounded so impressed or enthused.

"Better than last time?"

"Would I lie? This is incredible." He polished off the rest and held out his plate for more. "How'd you do it?"

Feeling as if she were floating on air she cut a generous second square, handed it to him, then licked chocolate off her thumb. "I switched to jumbo, fertilized eggs from a local farmer and I took your suggestion and used bittersweet and milk-chocolate chunks. Then I decreased the baking powder and…it's really not that interesting."

"Is to me."

She saw that he was sincere. "Well, I tinkered with the sugar and butter, soaked the cranberries in dark rum and slightly reduced the baking time. Do you think this recipe is good enough to take first place?"

"If the judges don't give you the blue ribbon, they're crazy. But, just to make sure they get that, you ought to call them out-of-this-world, blue-ribbon chocolate-chunk cranberry bars."

"That's exactly the name I've been searching for—very descriptive." Pleased, Fran gave a thumbs-up. "Thanks, Mitch."

"Anytime."

His gratified expression warmed her heart. As he carried his plate to the dishwasher she counted her blessings. Between perfecting the recipe and Mitch's fabulous name for them, she was so elated, she had to hug him.

"You're wonderful." She turned toward him with open arms.

Heat glittered in his eyes. "Don't tempt me."

He backed away, the right thing to do. How could she have forgotten? She locked her hands at her waist. "Well, thank you."

He gave a terse nod. "I'd best get back to work. Congratulations again on nailing that recipe."

He turned and walked out as if his life depended on getting away from her.

Nerves thrumming, Fran collapsed onto the very chair Mitch had used. The padded seat felt warm from his body. The battered recipe notes stared up at her. Blowing out a breath, she picked up a pen and shakily wrote Mitch's name for the bars at the top.

The recipe needed testing several more times. If every batch was as fantastic as this one, she would type out the final version and, following contest regulations, print out ten copies—five for each of the judges in the dessert category and five for the judges choosing the grand champion.

With so much to do, she would be way too busy to think about wanting Mitch.

FOR FRAN the next few days passed quickly. She was gone more than she was home and, aside from breakfast, she didn't see Mitch, who was holed up in his suite. Yet, she thought about him day and night, her love a living, growing thing.

Thank goodness he didn't realize. If he had any clue

how she felt, she was positive he'd check out today and never return. He certainly wouldn't be sitting at the counter after finagling coffee and another cranberry bar.

"I sure needed this break," Mitch said.

"Good, because I needed you to taste this batch. Is it better or worse than the other day?"

"The same." Mitch rubbed his flat belly. "And it's a winner."

And, to Fran's relief, it was. These were every bit as delicious as the other four batches she'd made since Saturday, proving that her recipe was reliable.

His plate empty, Mitch sipped coffee and watched while she packed for Saturday's bake-off, loading everything but the perishables into a large wicker basket.

"I'm confused," he said as he set down his mug. "Today's Thursday. The cook-off isn't until Saturday. Why pack up now?"

"Because with a houseful of guests checking in tomorrow, I might forget something. This way, everything is packed and ready." Even the butter, milk and the special eggs were in measured containers, ready to grab from the refrigerator Saturday morning.

"An organized woman," he said with admiration. An instant later, he frowned. "I'm not looking forward to all those people in here."

Fran wasn't, either. She wanted breakfasts with Mitch to herself and afternoons like this. There wasn't much time left and, when he checked out a week from Sunday, the Oceanside would feel empty, indeed.

"I know, but I'm thankful for the business. You have the whole top floor," she reminded him. "You don't have to mingle, even at breakfast." Though, if he gave that up, she'd probably never see him for more than a minute or two. At that sad thought, she bit her lip. "If you want, I'll set your breakfast aside and bring it up to your room."

"With your other guests, the cook-off and rest of the Cranberry Festival to worry about?" He shook his head. "You don't need to be fussing over me. I'll eat with everyone else."

"Okay, but, if you change your mind, let me know. For you, I truly don't mind."

He looked happy about that. "Well, *I* do, but thanks for offering. Tell me, Miss Organized, how are you planning to juggle feeding your guests Saturday *and* participating in the cook-off?"

She'd figured that out long ago. "The contest doesn't start until eleven and contestants can't get into the kitchen until ten forty-five. By then, breakfast will be long over. But, just in case, a woman who cleans for me sometimes offered to stop by and take care of the dishes. She'll work fast, too, because she wants to cheer me on."

"I'll be doing the same."

"You don't have to, Mitch," she said, knowing he needed every minute to write. "I know you want me to win. That's enough."

"The hell it is. I picked the name for those cranberry bars and it was my idea to use two kinds of chocolate. I'll be there for the surrogate thrills."

His support meant the world to her. "That'd be great."

As she closed the lid of the wicker basket, the front door buzzed.

Mitch groaned. "Don't tell me that's an early guest."

"Nobody's due until late tomorrow afternoon. I ordered new throw pillows for my sofa from an Internet catalog. Maybe they're here. But, just in case it's one of my cook-off competitors…" She stowed the pan of cranberry bars in the cabinet.

Leaving Mitch at the counter, she crossed the entry to the door. She opened it to find Cinnamon.

"Cinnamon. What a pleasant surprise." Fran gestured her inside. "What are you doing here??"

"My back's been bothering me all week and I've had some Braxton-Hicks—false labor—contractions," she said. "So Nick convinced me to start maternity leave now. A month before my due date! This morning was my last day at work, and they all shooed me out early." She gave a wry smile. "Wouldn't you know, I'm feeling pretty good now."

"I'm on Nick's side," Fran said.

"Me, too." Mitch, who no doubt had heard every word, strode across the entry. He and Cinnamon exchanged brief hello's—they'd met several times.

Glancing from Fran to Mitch, Cinnamon widened her eyes. "I hope I'm not interrupting anything?"

"I was helping Fran with something in the kitchen." Mitch winked at Fran.

Cinnamon sniffed the air. "Lucky you. What is that delicious aroma? Is that your contest recipe?"

Fran had sworn Mitch to secrecy, and now he eyed her with uncertainty. "Cinnamon's my best friend," she reminded him. "I can trust her. That's exactly what you smell, but don't tell a soul."

"I won't. Dessert category, right? If it tastes as fabulous as it smells, you're sure to win."

Since Cinnamon was here and had guessed the

category, why not let her sample a cranberry bar? "Would you like to try some with a cup of herbal tea?"

"I really can't. I need to stop at the cleaners and a few other places before Nick and I have our eight-month checkup at four. The reason I'm here is to wish you good luck now, before you get busy with a houseful of guests." She massaged her lower back. "On second thought, I will sit a minute and try that recipe. Just a small piece and a glass of water."

"I'll bring it to you," Fran said. "So sit yourself down in a nice, comfy chair in the great room."

"I'm so big now, that, once I'm in one of those soft chairs, I can't get out." Cinnamon shook her head. "Isn't that pathetic? A dining room or kitchen chair is better."

Pressing the heels of her hands on her lower back, she lumbered slowly into the kitchen. She stopped in the threshold between the kitchen and dining room. "My back." Leaning heavily on the serving counter, she winced. "It's killing me."

Her suddenly pinched, pale face alarmed Fran. Mitch looked equally worried.

"Forget four o'clock," he said. "You need to see your doctor right now."

Fran nodded. "I'm calling Nick."

"Please don't." Cinnamon shot her a pleading look. "He's overly protective as it is. This is what's been happening all week. Once I rest a while, I'll be fine."

While Fran pulled a chair from the table, Mitch held her arm and helped her toward it.

Before she sat down, she hesitated, a funny look on her face. "Oh, no! I think my water just broke."

Fran stared at the liquid trickling down her panty-hose. "But it's too early." She exchanged a panicked look with Mitch.

"Apparently, Callie's too impatient to wait. Nick was right, she's coming early." Cupping her belly, Cinnamon bit her lip. "I'm scared!" Tears filled her eyes. "Could you get my cell phone out of my purse?"

"It'll be all right," Mitch said. "You can make calls while I bring my car around."

"You call Nick on your cell and I'll phone the hospital." Fran hurried to the kitchen phone.

By the time Fran finished and Cinnamon slipped her cell phone into her purse half a minute later, Mitch was back.

"Nick isn't answering," she said. "I left a message."

"We'll find him. Right now, the hospital's expecting us." Fran clasped one arm and Mitch took the other. "Let's go."

"I parked as close as I could to the steps. Can you make it, or do you want me to carry you?"

"Right now, I probably weigh nearly as much as you. I'll walk, but very slowly," Cinnamon said, clenching her teeth.

Before they moved five feet, she gasped. "It's too late! The baby's coming." Moaning, with Fran and Mitch's help, she sank to the floor.

Dear God. Terrified, Fran looked to Mitch. "What should we do?"

He already had his cell phone out. "Call 9-1-1 and get help."

Chapter Eleven

With his cell on speakerphone, crouched on the kitchen floor, Mitch supported Cinnamon's head and shoulders and followed Jennifer, the female 9-1-1 operator's, instructions. Wearing a clean bib apron, Fran knelt at the edge of the towel draped over Cinnamon's middle and bent knees. Her face radiated calm and no doubt reassured Cinnamon. But, when she glanced at Mitch, her eyes flashed fear. Mitch was scared, too, and totally out of his comfort zone. Thank God for the woman on the other end of the phone.

Per her directions, he and Fran had spread a clean sheet under Cinnamon. They'd thoroughly washed their hands, Fran up to her elbows. Mitch had set a pot of water on the stove to boil, adding tongs, several lengths of string, scissors and a turkey baster for dealing with the umbilical cord and suctioning the baby's mouth. The baby was coming fast—according to the operator unusually fast for a first birth—and he hoped to God the ambulance hurried.

"Don't you dare look at my privates, Mitch Matthews," Cinnamon ordered, tipping her head up to offer a stern frown.

As if he could avoid looking in that direction. "I swear, I can't see much except the towel," he said. Which was the truth.

"Fran, can you see the head yet?" the operator, Jennifer, asked.

"I think so, but only the hair."

Mitch noted her awed expression and almost wished he, too, could see.

"That's called crowning."

"I learned about that in childbir—" Cinnamon stopped as a contraction gripped her. "I need to push!" she cried through gritted teeth.

"Not just yet," the operator said. "I want you to put your head back and pant. Can you help her with that, Mitch?"

He had no idea what she was talking about. "Yeah, if you tell me what to do."

"Hold on to her and encourage her to pant. Fran—"

"I need to push!" Cinnamon shouted.

Mitch held her firmly. "Put your head back, look at me and pant." To his relief, she obeyed, her eyes locked on his.

"She's doing it," Fran said.

"Good job," Jennifer replied. "Fran, what do you see now?"

"More of the head."

"Nothing else?"

"Not yet."

"All right, you can push now, Cinnamon," Jennifer instructed. "When the next urge comes, I want you to hold on to Mitch's forearms, tuck your chin and go for it, just the way you learned in childbirth class."

"Okay." Cinnamon moaned. "Here I go."

She squeezed his forearms so hard, he winced. Sweat trickled down her brow and her face turned red as she bent to Mother Nature's will. When the urge passed, she fell back and rested. Not a minute later, the whole thing started again. Six times before Fran smiled.

"The baby's head is out."

Mitch saw it, too, a tiny, wet head with dark hair. A stunning sight that would have paralyzed him with all that it symbolized if he'd had time to think.

"I want you to cup that head, Fran, to keep it safe and supported. Tell me, which way is it turned?"

"To the left."

"Then the left shoulder will be born first."

"It's happening again." Grabbing hold of Mitch in a fresh death-grip, Cinnamon tucked her chin, grunted and pushed hard.

"One shoulder's out," Fran said.

"Next time she pushes, gently pull straight up until the other shoulder is born."

Cinnamon pushed again. Amazed by the miracle he was witnessing, Mitch saw the second shoulder emerge.

Fran caught his eye. The raw emotion that passed between them was deeper and more heartfelt than anything he'd ever experienced.

A scant minute later, the baby slid into Fran's hands. "Your daughter has arrived," she said in a voice laced with wonder. "And she is beautiful. Welcome to the world, little Callie."

Mitch thought she was skinny and looked like an ugly old man, but beautiful, all the same.

"Is she okay? Let me see her." Cinnamon struggled to sit up.

"Congratulations," Jennifer said. "Keep her head supported. Mitch, grab that turkey baster you cooled down and suction out her mouth."

After quickly following Jennifer's instructions the baby let out a lusty cry. Fran held her up for Cinnamon.

"Oh, God." Cinnamon wept.

Overcome himself, Mitch blinked. Hunkering down he kissed Cinnamon's forehead. "Good work."

"Still supporting the baby's head, Fran? I want you to wrap her with that summer blanket you found, but leave her belly exposed."

Fran did, and the baby looked around with slow, jerky movements.

"Now for the cord," Jennifer said.

He was about to cut it when the wailing sound of a siren grew louder. Suddenly, Nick burst through the door. "Where is she?"

"We're in the kitchen," Cinnamon called out.

Nick sprinted into the room, his face a mixture of fear and joy. "Are you all right?" he asked, kneeling beside his wife.

Cinnamon beamed. "You're just in time to meet your daughter."

SOMEHOW THE AFTERNOON faded into night. As Fran and Mitch cleaned up after the ambulance took the proud new parents and little Callie to the hospital, she shook her head. "We delivered a baby." She dried her hands on a kitchen towel, then handed it to Mitch. "Right here in this kitchen."

"As life experiences go, I'd have to say this ranks right on top." He hung up the towel. "I don't think I'll ever be the same."

"No, and for that I feel so blessed."

"Yeah," he replied, the single word potent with feeling.

The incredulous, tender look in his eyes was new and matched Fran's own wonder. A bond had been forged between them that no one else ever would share.

She smiled. "If you hadn't been here to help… Well, I'm just glad you were."

"Ditto. You could've been out, running errands. Then what would I have done?"

He looked so horrified, Fran laughed. "Would you like a glass of wine? I would."

She would sip it slowly, so as not to overdo.

He nodded. "And something to eat. Delivering a baby works up a man's appetite. What should we order for dinner?"

After what they had shared, eating together felt right and necessary. Fran's heart simply was too full to be alone. "We don't have to order out," she said. "There are salad greens in the crisper and a frozen lasagna casserole in the freezer. I'll make garlic bread and we'll eat in front of the fireplace in the great room. How does that sound?"

"Terrific. You take care of the casserole and the bread, and I'll make the salad and start the fire."

An hour later, wine sipped and dinner over, Fran still was awed over Callie's birth. And by the profound connection she felt with Mitch. She needed his company tonight, and he seemed to feel the same way. After clearing the dishes, they returned together to the great room.

Taking hold of her hand, he pulled her to the love seat. Beyond caring that touching him was dangerous, Fran welcomed his arm around her shoulders. The only light in the room came from the blazing fire, and beyond the glass-to-ceiling windows, the world was black. As if there were nothing outside this room.

In comfortable silence, they watched the crackling fire.

"Most people never share what we did," she said.

"They sure don't. I'm thinking about how to incorporate the experience into the book. Something about how life itself is a miracle and our awareness of that fact heightens our gratitude. That, without gratitude, there is no bliss."

"That sounds like something the wise Mitch Matthews would say." Fran smiled at him.

"It does, doesn't it?" He was quiet a moment, watching the fire. Then he angled his head to look at her. "Aside from winning the contest, what do you want out of life, Fran?"

Delivering Cinnamon's baby had only heightened her craving for her own child. "Love," she replied without hesitation. In particular, Mitch's love. But even as close as she felt to him, she couldn't admit that. "A husband and several children. But I already told you that."

"You did. You'll make a great mother."

His eyes were warm with feeling, but Fran was no fool. He liked her, nothing more. And, anyway, tonight there was no room in her heart or her head for wishful thinking.

"Do you think you'll ever get married, Mitch?" A question she wouldn't normally ask, but now…

"Since my father died, I've thought about it a lot. But I'm thirty-seven years old and haven't fallen in love yet. I'm not sure I ever will." One shoulder shrugged. "I'd have to find a woman who can live with that."

"That wouldn't be a happy marriage. You'd probably end up divorced."

"Exactly. Though I don't think my parents loved each other, and they managed all right."

"But were they *happy?*"

He looked pensive. "Since my mother died when I was ten, I don't really know. But, from what I remember, I'd have to say, no."

The fire crackled and hissed, and Fran absorbed this interesting glimpse into Mitch's past. His childhood couldn't have been much fun.

As for finding a woman willing to marry without love, a wealthy, handsome man like Mitch would have no trouble finding one.

It would not be Fran. She'd never settle for a loveless marriage. Yet, here she was, in love with Mitch. That was an entirely depressing thought, but this was not the time for low spirits.

"Isn't my little goddaughter cute?" she asked, returning to a cheerier subject.

"I wouldn't go that far. To me, she looked like George Burns with hair." His mouth quirked. "And so tiny. I never realized how puny and skinny babies are."

"Most are bigger and weigh more. Don't forget, Callie was a month early. We're lucky her lungs were developed enough to work on their own. Otherwise…" Fran shuddered at the possibilities.

"Hey. She's fine." Mitch cupped her face and looked deeply into her eyes. "The medics said so, and so did Cinnamon when you called the hospital. You'll see for yourself when you visit tomorrow, so stop worrying." He kissed the tip of her nose.

Fran snuggled against him, her head on his chest. She heard the steady thud of his heart. Cuddled together this way felt comfortable and natural—or would if she could take down her braid.

Craning her head back she glanced up at Mitch. "Mind if I take down my hair?"

"I'd like to see it down."

Pulling out of his grasp she removed the tie that secured her hair, then unplaited the braid. When she finished she combed her fingers through her hair, then shook her head. Her hair fell down her back and over her shoulders, loose and free. That felt good.

"You have beautiful hair," Mitch said. "May I touch it?"

The heat smoldering in his eyes fanned her own desire. With or without his love, tonight was about comfort and closeness. Wordless, she nodded.

His fingers lifted and combed through the strands with gentle reverence. "So thick and soft."

It was only hair, yet his touch felt both as private and intimate as a lover's caress…something between the two of them and no one else. Savoring the attention, Fran closed her eyes. Suddenly his warm breath caressed her face, and she knew he'd moved closer.

She opened her eyes to find him watching her through a heavy-lidded gaze that melted her.

"Right now, I feel so close to you," she murmured.

"I want to feel even closer, as close as two people can be." His hands continued to fondle her hair. "I want to make love with you."

It was what she'd longed for and fought against, for what seemed like forever. Tonight, longing won out—regardless what tomorrow brought.

"I want the same thing," she whispered.

"I was tested a month ago. I'm clean."

"I haven't been with anyone in a while, and I know I'm healthy, too."

Tipping up her chin he searched her face. "If we do this, our relationship will change in ways we can't anticipate."

Not for Fran. She already loved him. The danger lay with him, how he'd feel about her after. But she wanted him too much to let her fear intrude. "I don't care. Tonight, I need to be with you."

He opened his mouth to speak. She placed her finger against his lips. "Don't say anything, Mitch. Just love me."

Stretching upward she kissed him with all the feeling inside her. A long, openmouthed, tongue-tangling kiss. When it ended, they both were breathing harder.

Mitch pulled her sideways onto his lap, his kisses eager and deep and searching. Fran lost herself in his taste, his smell, the feel of his silky hair under her palms. Between her legs, she was damp and needy, hungry for more.

His arousal pressed against her bottom. Craving it someplace else, she attempted to straddle him. Her long legs and the small love seat made that impossible.

"Let's move to a more comfortable place," Mitch said. "Are you on the pill?"

She shook her head. "Since I'm not seeing anyone, there's no reason to be."

"I always carry protection, but it's upstairs. Let's go."

Too impatient to move that far, Fran shook her head. "It's so romantic by the fire and the rug is soft and thick." She moved off his lap to the floor. "Lots of men carry condoms in their wallets."

"I do, but it's old." He lifted his hip, slid out his wallet and retrieved a packet. Holding it up to the light he studied it. "The foil's still intact. I guess it'll do."

He joined Fran on the floor, wrapped his arms around her and kissed her again.

SITTING ON THE FLOOR with Fran's long legs wrapped around his waist and the sweetest part of her wriggling mercilessly against his groin, Mitch feared he'd lose control and embarrass himself.

But control was his forte and, so far, he'd managed to hang on to it. That wouldn't change, even with Fran. Especially not with Fran.

"Let's get naked," he said, untangling her legs and scooting out from under her.

Fran nodded. Her mouth was swollen from his kisses and the sultry look on her face made him hot to push her back and bury himself in her sweetness. Now.

Easy, he counseled himself. He wanted this to be good for her, too. After longing for her for weeks, he could afford to be patient a little longer.

Facing him on the floor, with only the fire to light the

darkness, she lifted the hem of her shirt and pulled it over her head. Mitch did the same with his. Seconds later her bra was off.

She tossed her head and her lovely, dark hair spilled over her shoulders and breasts. Sweet heaven, she was sexy. With hands that trembled he traced a lock as far as her nipple, smiling as Fran caught her breath.

He lifted her hair and draped it over her shoulders. Her lovely breasts stood proud and visible, the pointed nipples begging attention. His thumbs teased both sensitive tips. Fran moaned, and they tightened still more.

Positioning her thighs over his, he bowed his head and thoroughly laved and suckled each of her breasts until she was squirming and panting and needy. *His.*

"Should I stop?" he teased, raising his head.

"You'd better not." Her own hands cupped her breasts, an offering to him.

"Touching yourself." He growled with pleasure. "Do you know what that does to me?" He molded his hands over hers and kneaded her breasts.

Then pulled her hands away and grazed his teeth over each taut point.

Fran hissed in a breath. Afraid he'd hurt her, he stilled. "Too rough?"

She shook her head. "Do it again."

Her eagerness only heightened his hunger. Blood roared in his head as he nipped and suckled and teased until he was half-crazed with the taste of her.

As if she sensed that he was near the breaking point, she cupped his face and raised his head. "My turn."

She leaned forward. Licked and kissed his chest. His

ribs. His belly, her hot mouth promising heaven and driving him wild and mindless.

"No more until we're naked," he gasped, stopping her. He unwrapped her legs, then stood and helped her up.

Looking dazed and hungry, her gaze locked on his, Fran unbuttoned her cords, slid the zipper down and shimmied out of her pants…a striptease Mitch never would forget.

"Now you," she said.

He kicked out of his jeans. Eyed her panties. "Those must go."

"And your boxers."

In seconds, they stood naked before each other. Catching hold of her hands he studied her. In the firelight her skin glowed and her hair shimmered. "I've never seen a more luscious, beautiful woman," he said.

"I wish I didn't have the extra fat around my hips and stomach."

"What extra fat? You're perfect."

"And you're huge." Wide-eyed she stared at his hard-on.

"For you. Lie with me."

Together they sank onto the floor. Half on top of her, Mitch captured her mouth with his. She clasped his shoulders, pulling him tight against her breasts. Levering up on one arm, he slid his free hand down the smooth skin of her belly, then to the soft thatch between her legs.

She parted them and his hand moved lower, to where she was slick with need. She caught her breath. He fingered her until she squirmed.

And he had to taste her most sensitive place. He kissed his way down her navel, stopping at her thatch. Lifting her hips, she wordlessly summoned him.

His heart pounding, he parted her folds and licked her tiny, honeyed nub until she moaned and shifted restlessly.

"Mitch," she said, sounding as if she'd just run a race. "I'm about to…to…"

He was most comfortable this way, holding on to his own control while his partner lost hers. "Let go, Fran."

He swirled his tongue around her pleasure center and inserted two fingers into her moist passage.

Frenzied, making wild sounds deep in her throat, she came undone. When she finished, Mitch kissed her inner thigh and lay down beside her.

Fran sighed and smiled languidly into his eyes. "That was… Well, there are no words."

Aside from delivering the baby, pleasuring Fran was the most remarkable moment of his life. "It was amazing." He kissed her forehead.

She glanced at his arousal, then bit her lip. "What about you, Mitch?"

Though his body throbbed for release, he sensed that she wanted to be held. "We have all night," he said. "We'll get to me later."

He settled her close to his side. Seconds later her breathing slowed, and he knew she'd fallen asleep. He carefully extricated himself from her arms, then grabbed the afghan from the sectional. Returning to her side he covered them both.

Chapter Twelve

Fran had no idea how long she'd slept, but she woke with Mitch holding her close and the fire burned to embers. By the sound of his breathing, he was asleep.

This had been a day of miracles. First the baby, now this... She smiled at the wonder of it.

An instant later, her smile faded. The man she loved had satisfied her without thinking of himself. Now she would pleasure him. Her hand crept to his groin.

Within moments he was huge and hard and devouring her mouth with his while his clever fingers ramped up the fire in her body.

"Your turn," she gasped, pulling away.

She moved down his body, letting her hair caress and tease his nipples and abdomen. When she reached his navel, he sucked in his belly. Pushing her hair out of the way, she touched her tongue to his swollen head. His hips jerked upward. Groaning, he cupped the back of her head. She took him deep into her mouth. But only for a moment.

Suddenly, she was on her back and he was poised over her, his arousal teasing the part of her that most craved him.

"Are you ready?" he asked, his voice tight with strain.

"Please," she whispered, tilting her hips toward him.

Then mercifully, he was inside her, stretching and filling her with his heat. She wrapped her legs around his waist.

He pushed deep, then stilled. "Does that feel okay?"

In response, she squeezed her muscles around him. "More, Mitch. Hurry."

Thrusting hard and easing back, again and again, faster and faster, he brought her closer to the brink. Tension coiled and built inside her, and her world narrowed to the place where their bodies joined. Another thrust pushed her over the edge.

As her climax built her world trembled, shook and flipped upside down.

"Fran," Mitch called out, joining her and pushing so deep inside her, she no longer knew where she ended and he began.

When her brain began to function again and her heart stopped pounding, she kissed his chest. "You're a fantastic lover, Mitch." *And I love you.*

"So are you." He pulled her close. After a while, he squeezed her hip with his warm palm. "We should go to bed now, where it's comfortable. Your place or mine?"

"You have the bigger bed," Fran said.

He pulled her up. Hand in hand, they headed upstairs. Once in his bed, he curled spoon-style behind her.

Spending the night with Mitch was more than she'd ever dreamed of. Even though he'd never love her, for tonight, making love was enough.

MITCH WOKE UP. It was still dark outside and he was in his bed, molded to Fran's backside. The flowery smell of her hair filled his senses and, underneath that, her woman scent.

Aroused and hungry to make love with her again, he pushed her hair aside and kissed the sensitive place where her neck met her shoulder. He stroked her hip, then slid his hand up and cupped her breast.

Murmuring she turned to him. With a drowsy, sexy smile she draped her thigh over his hip, bringing her sensitive center flush against his arousal. Heat raged through him. He would plumb the depths of her sweetness, but not without protection.

Protection. They'd forgotten to use it earlier. Swearing, he untangled himself and pulled away from her. He groped for the lamp on the bedside table and flipped it on, blinking in the sudden light. The clock said 2:00 a.m. He sat up.

"Mitch? What's happened?" Pulling the covers with her Fran sat up beside him.

"Downstairs in front of the fire—I didn't use a condom."

"I never even realized… Oh, no." Alarm erased the sleepy softness from her face. "I can't believe it. I guess since we'd been asleep we weren't thinking."

"That's no excuse. I'm not a careless man—usually." Mitch never had forgotten before. Had never lost himself in a woman before, either.

What had happened to the control he valued so highly? He didn't understand his feelings for Fran and sure wasn't about to figure things out right now. Not without time to think and analyze. He sure as hell didn't know what he'd do if she ended up pregnant.

Shaken and cursing his lapse of control, he scrubbed

a hand over his face. "Where are you in your monthly cycle?"

"Very near the end. If there's a safe time, this is it. I should be okay."

Mitch wasn't a praying man, but he prayed she was right. Clasping the sheet and comforter under her arms, with her hair falling over her shoulders and breasts and her face flushed and open, Fran certainly looked unconcerned. And very sexy.

Even as scared as he was, he wanted her more than ever. He must be out of his mind.

But if they used protection... "Why don't I get that box of condoms from the dresser."

"Why don't you," Fran said.

In seconds, the box was open on the night table and Mitch's body was primed and ready. He made love with Fran again, this time fully protected.

WHEN FRAN KNOCKED on the door of Cinnamon's hospital room midmorning Friday, Cinnamon lay stretched out peacefully atop her neatly made-up bed, wearing designer loungewear. Her eyes were closed and she looked serene and peaceful, not at all like the hot-faced, straining woman who had given birth on Fran's kitchen floor less than twenty-four hours ago. Cuddled beside her, the tiny bundle that was Callie also slept.

Mother and child, Fran's best friend and goddaughter. Love filled her heart, too much of it for envy.

And she and Mitch had participated in the miraculous and joyful event of Callie's birth, then shared their own private joy. Her already full heart overflowed and tears sprang to her eyes.

Cinnamon stirred and awakened. "Hi," she said softly. "Come in. Are those flowers for me?"

Smiling through her tears, Fran held up the pot of fall blooming crocuses, yellow waxbells and burgundy asters. "Of course," she replied in an equally low voice that hopefully wouldn't disturb Callie. "Except for the crocus, they're all fall perennials you can transplant into your garden."

"How thoughtful. Thanks. Why are you crying?"

Fran shook her head. "I'm just so filled with happiness that it's leaking from my eyes."

Cinnamon teared up, too. "I know what you mean."

Much as Fran wanted to stay and visit, she knew Cinnamon needed rest. "You're tired. Why don't I come back later."

"I'm fine, and way too excited to sleep." Cinnamon gave her daughter an adoring look, cuddled her close, then carefully sat up. "They kept Callie in the preemie ward all night to make sure she was okay, so I slept quite a bit. I didn't get her to myself until this morning. Isn't she something?" Yawning, she gestured Fran over.

Still cradling the planter Fran peered at Callie. Since yesterday, her little features had become more pronounced and the tuft of dark hair on her head looked soft and fine as sewing thread.

Tenderness washed through her, and she had a longing for a baby of her own someday. "She's something special. I'd like to hold my goddaughter. Where should I put the flowers?"

She glanced at the vases filling every spare space, a testament to Cinnamon's many friends. "Gosh, you have enough here to open your own florist shop."

"There's room on the windowsill. You just missed Nick. He slept in this narrow bed with me last night— can you imagine? He went home to shower, change clothes and pick up some things for me. I expect Sharon, Abby and Andy will be here soon."

"Then, it's a good thing I'm here now, because I want the two of you to myself for a while. Now, give me that baby." Fran held out her arms.

"Be sure to support her head," Cinnamon cautioned.

Holding the tiny baby, who weighed less than the plant she'd brought, Fran moved cautiously to a beige armchair and sat down. A fresh wave of emotion flooded her. "She's so little and sweet. Absolutely beautiful. How's she doing?"

"For a baby born four weeks early, very well. But the doctor wants to keep her here until Sunday, just to make sure nothing unexpected crops up. I'll be staying, too."

The baby stirred. Her tiny rosebud mouth pursed before returning to slackness. Both Fran and Cinnamon stared in fascination.

"How's Mitch holding up?" Cinnamon asked after a moment. "It's not every day a man helps deliver a baby."

"He's doing really well." Fran knew she was blushing. "He asked me to congratulate you again."

Earlier, they'd made love in the soaker tub in his suite and against the serving counter, a breakfast Fran never would forget. After satisfying her thoroughly, Mitch had headed whistling upstairs to work on the book. With guests due to arrive this afternoon, she probably wouldn't see him alone again, a thought that dimmed her joy.

"You're glowing, Fran and there's a love bite on your neck. Yet, you're also frowning." Cinnamon arched her eyebrows curiously. "What happened between you and Mitch?"

Someone knocked on the door. Grateful for the interruption—Fran wasn't sure how much to share—she jumped up. "I'll get that."

"Flowers for Cinnamon Mahoney," said the delivery boy, who was built like a high-school football player. The colorful bouquet in his arms was huge. "Where do you want these?" he said.

"On the floor, under the window."

"Is there a card?" Cinnamon asked after the boy left. "Will you read it?"

Fran passed Callie to her mother, then slipped the envelope from the holder. "It's from Mitch. 'Welcome to the world, Callie. Good work, Cinnamon. Best wishes and thanks for an unforgettable experience—Mitch.'"

"That's so dear of him," Cinnamon said.

Fran agreed. He was so thoughtful, and she loved him so much.

"Now, sit back down and tell me what happened."

Why not? Cinnamon was Fran's best friend. Besides, she needed to talk to somebody. She glanced at the sleeping baby and lowered her voice.

"We were both so awed by Callie's birth. When you participate in a miracle it binds you together. One thing led to another, and… We made love," she finished, her cheeks hot.

"I had a hunch that would happen."

"You did?"

Cinnamon nodded. "I saw the way you looked at each other over me."

"You were having a baby. How could you notice anything?"

"There were moments between contractions when there wasn't much else to do but observe the two people helping me. I definitely sensed something between you two. So? Is he a good lover?"

"Fantastic." Fran saw no reason to mention that they'd forgotten to use protection the first time. With her period due to start tomorrow she was sure she was safe.

"Okay, I know why you're glowing. But why do I sense sadness underneath?"

"Because, with a house full of guests, we won't be able to make love again before Mitch leaves."

"Why not? If you're careful no one will know."

"I can't take that risk. Sleeping with a guest—well, that would look terrible."

"You could meet someplace outside town."

Not with Mitch needing every waking minute to finish his book. And not with her period. Fran shook her head. "The other problem is, I'm in love with him."

"Why is that a problem?"

"You know how he is, Cinnamon. He doesn't fall in love."

"Well, he sure as heck *likes* you. A lot."

"I know, and I am thankful for that." Fran sighed. "Anyway, he'll be leaving a week from Sunday. Then it'll be over between us." And he would leave without ever knowing how she truly felt.

"Not necessarily. He could come down anytime, and you can go up there."

"It's a nine-hour drive, which makes visiting a real chore. Even if we flew, it's a four-hour drive from here to the Portland airport and another hour in the air."

"So? You're two intelligent people. I'm sure you can work it out."

"Mitch hasn't said anything."

"Maybe he will."

And maybe not. "I'm not holding my breath."

Cinnamon bit her lip. "I'm sorry, Fran."

"Don't be. I knew what I was getting in to." She'd never forget the ecstasy of making love with Mitch and never would regret it. And now was no time to think about this. She forced a smile. "Hey, you just had a baby. There's no room right now for anything but joy."

Callie began to stir and make funny little noises. Cinnamon shot her a tender smile. "She's waking up."

A nurse knocked on the door, then bustled in. "It's time to change and feed little Callie."

"They want me to breast-feed often, to stimulate my milk and help her learn to suck," Cinnamon said. "She gets a bottle, too."

"Then I'll leave you to it." Fran stood. "My guests will be arriving soon, and I should get back."

"Enjoy, and good luck at the cook-off," Cinnamon said as she rose and carried Callie to the changing table provided by the hospital.

"Thanks. I'll try to visit afterward and let you know how I did."

"You'll have a house full of guests. Don't worry, I'll hear about it. Or call if you want. Better yet, wait a few days and then come to the house." She winked. "And bring me some of your entry."

"Will do." Fran kissed her best friend's cheek, blew a kiss at Callie and headed home.

Chapter Thirteen

Mitch whistled as he shaved Saturday morning. Despite the guests sure to be at the table and having had only three hours' sleep, he felt alive and energized. Happy, even. A new man. He studied his reflection, noting the sparkle in his eyes, and grinned at himself.

It was a miraculous change he owed partly to Foster, but more so to Fran. Through her unbridled passion she'd proved his father wrong. Losing yourself in the right person was a sign of trust, not weakness, and the past little while had been an eye-opening, unforgettable life lesson. He wiped his face with a towel and padded to the dresser in the bedroom. Now that he truly had experienced his own passion, he couldn't believe he'd held himself back all these years.

And it wasn't just a one-night fluke, either. They'd proved that yesterday. Twice. First with hot sex in the soaker tub. Then against the serving counter, after a hearty breakfast.

Mitch stepped into clean boxers, pulled a T-shirt over his head and grinned again. Later, Fran had left to visit Cinnamon while he, sated and relaxed, had holed up in his room. He'd written like a man possessed. The words had poured out, and he had no doubt that the flood would continue.

He knew with certainty that he would finish the book on time, and couldn't wait to share the good news with Fran. If he hurried, he'd make it to the kitchen ahead of the other guests for a few precious minutes alone with her. He pulled on jeans and a sweater.

Anticipation hummed through him and a certain part of his body stirred. He shook his head. "No sex for you today."

Not with all those people in the house and the cook-off today.

Despite his rapidly approaching deadline he intended to show up and cheer for Fran. Then it was back to work, maybe 'round the clock. He wouldn't think about making love with her again until he finished the book, which worked out well, since she refused to sleep with him with guests in the house. A whole week of abstinence. Dismal.

He sat down and shoved his feet into socks. Next Sunday, they'd all be gone. Then he'd leave, too. That put a damper on Mitch's excellent mood. This was where he wanted to be, the place where he felt most at home. He wasn't about to analyze that. It simply was.

Toeing into his sneakers he thought about staying an extra night or two after that. Yeah, that'd do the trick. He was certain Fran wouldn't mind, and would talk to her about it this morning. He glanced at his watch. There wasn't much time before the others showed up for breakfast. Best hurry.

As he headed downstairs he heard voices in the dining room. No time alone with Fran, after all. Disappointed, he found a seat at the table, facing the kitchen. It was a crisp, unusually sunny morning for late October, but Mitch wasn't interested in the view outside. His attention fixed on Fran. She was dressed in an emerald-green sweater and skirt, a white apron protecting her from cooking mishaps. A matching green ribbon secured the end of her braid.

Her turtleneck sweater didn't quite hide the love bite he'd marked her with. His body stirred yet again. "'Morning," he said in a low, gruff voice.

"Good morning."

Warmth and desire shimmered in her eyes before she gestured around the table with introductions. "This is Mitch Matthews. He's been here a month."

He recognized several familiar faces from previous years and greeted them.

The small talk began while he helped himself to juice, cheese soufflé and sausage patties. The Olivers, a silver-haired couple across the table, asked why he'd been here so long.

"I needed a break from Seattle," he said.

Several of his tablemates shot speculative glances at him and then at Fran, who was too busy to notice.

"And I've been working on a project," he added, in case they wondered later why he spent most of his time upstairs.

"For anyone who doesn't know, Mitch writes motivational books," Mrs. Oliver said. "Are you working on another one?"

Fran shot him a curious look, probably wondering

what he'd say. She didn't yet know that this book was practically writing itself. Mitch wasn't about to talk about that in front of the other guests.

"Not exactly." He directed them to his Web site for updates and information. Tired of being the focus of attention he glanced around the table. "Did Fran mention this morning's cook-off?"

"She certainly did," said Nina Gaines, one of the guests Mitch had met before.

The table buzzed with expectation.

"I can't believe the Food Network is filming it," Nina said. "I'm so excited that I'll be there, watching the whole thing! It's at Town Hall, right?"

"That's where the judging is," Fran said. "We'll be using the kitchens at various restaurants in town to prepare our dishes—under the watchful eyes of Food Network staff to make sure no one cheats. They'll be filming that, too."

At the far end of the table, a blonde named Patty O'-Callahan, who was here with her husband, Bryan, eyed Fran. "Are you nervous? I would be."

Fran shrugged. "A little."

Fran, nervous? She was calm and easygoing. That was one of the attributes that drew Mitch to her. Except when she was hungry and writhing under him… He liked her even more then. Smiling to himself, he grabbed his cold juice and drained the glass.

"Do you think you'll win the ten thousand dollars?" Nina asked.

"Well, first I need to win in my category. If I do, I'll be up against the four other category winners. The winner of that round gets the check, an interview with the

Food Network and publication of the winning recipe. So think positive thoughts for me."

"We will," Mrs. Oliver said.

"Even more important, do we get to taste your entry for breakfast?" Bryan guffawed.

"It's not a breakfast food," Fran said.

"Is it dinner dish, or maybe a drink?" Patty asked. "Or, ooh—a dessert?"

"That's confidential. But, once the contest is over, I promise to serve the dish to everyone." Fran piled food onto the seagulls' plates.

"Her recipe is a sure thing," Mitch said. "I helped her taste test it, so I should know."

Another round of speculative glances followed.

"How come *you* rate?" Nina asked.

"Just lucky, I guess."

Fran flushed, and Mitch knew she remembered the other things he'd tasted. He wanted her more than ever.

Not for another eight days. It seemed like forever.

FIFTEEN MINUTES before the official start of the cook-off, standing at her "station" in the gleaming commercial kitchen of the town bakery, Fran searched frantically through her basket of supplies. For all her careful planning, she'd been so distracted by Mitch, she'd forgotten the eggs.

Upset, she approached the proctor, a slim, fiftysomething male with a Food Network logo in his jacket. "I've forgotten my eggs. What can I do?"

"Anything, just as long as you're ready to go in—" he glanced at the wall clock "—fifteen minutes. Otherwise…" He made a slashing gesture across his throat.

There wasn't time to go home, get the eggs and drive back. Panic tightened Fran's stomach. She glanced at the other contestants sharing the space. Joelle and Noelle were stationed to one side of her and Corinne Rogers, a friendly, middle-aged woman who taught sixth grade at Cranberry Grade and High School, took the other side. There were four more contestants, people she recognized but didn't personally know.

Ignoring the cameraman setting up for filming and thinking about how she could adjust her recipe to compensate for smaller eggs, she hurried toward the twins. "Do you have extra eggs? I've forgotten mine."

To her dismay, they shook their heads. It was the same with Corinne.

"Does anyone here have extra eggs?" she asked, raising her voice.

Not a one of them. What to do?

Noelle patted her arm. "Call someone, dear."

"Good idea."

Digging her cell phone out of her purse, Fran tried Mitch's cell. She only hoped he hadn't turned it off.

He picked up on the second ring. "Fran? Where are you?"

"Thank goodness you answered. I'm at the bakery, and I forgot the eggs. The ones I drove across town to get? They're in the fridge, packed in a plastic container. If I don't have them in thirteen minutes, I'll have to drop out of the contest."

"Hang tight. I'll be there ASAP."

Since there was nothing to do now—the rules stipulated contestants could unpack supplies but nothing more until the official start of the contest—Fran watched the clock with mounting tension. But getting uptight would only make things worse. Trying to calm herself, she thought about Mitch and this morning.

Since Friday afternoon they hadn't had a single moment alone together, except this morning, when he'd helped carry some of her things into the garage. He'd wished her good luck and had repeated his belief that she would win. She'd asked about the book and he'd filled her in. He was writing nonstop and expected to finish on time. If that wasn't enough good news, he'd asked to stay a few extra nights so that they could be together. Then he'd kissed her, his mouth hungry and full of promise. She'd melted on the spot.

Her gaze returned to the clock. With only two minutes left, not even the warm memories helped. She was a mass of nerves and thought she might throw up.

Suddenly Mitch strode into the kitchen—tall and handsome and, today, her savior.

All attention turned to him, but his focus was fixed on Fran.

"Did I make it in time?" he asked, handing her the container.

"Yes." Tears of relief filled her eyes. "Thank you."

He tipped up her chin. "Hey, this is no time for crying. You have a contest to win."

How she loved this man. Smiling and blinking, she nodded. "You're right."

"That's my girl." He kissed her, a light, quick brush of the lips that filled her with warmth and promise. "Good luck, and see you later."

With thirty seconds to go, Fran set the eggs beside the other ingredients.

Noelle and Joelle glanced at her, both of them with sly smiles.

"Well, well," Noelle said. "Looks as if Alice Caroline's chocolates and a month of living alone with Mitch worked wonders."

Joelle nodded. "We heard about you and him delivering Cinnamon's baby. That must've been quite an experience."

"It was," Fran said. "Something I'll never forget."

"It certainly would bring people close. Are you two an item now?" Noelle asked, arching her eyebrows over the rims of her glasses.

How would Mitch answer that? "We're friends," Fran answered honestly. And lovers. But that was nobody's business.

"The way he looks at you…" Joelle scoffed.

"His feelings are too warm for mere friendship," Noelle said with a sly look. "I'm thinking you two are sleeping together."

"Noelle!" Fran's cheeks burned.

A buzzer sounded. "Gather round, people," the proctor said.

Fran, the twins, Corinne and the others formed a semicircle in front of him. The cameraman moved in behind them, video camera pointed and ready.

"I'm Mark Todd and I'll be watching you work this morning. There are seven commercial kitchens in greater Cranberry, each with five contestants, a cameraman and a proctor such as myself. That's thirty-five contestants from the greater Cranberry area, cooking in five categories. Appetizers, breads, main dishes, beverages and desserts. To keep things interesting, we've mixed up the groups. None of the people in this room are in the same category."

"Reminds me of standardized tests they give in schools," Corinne said to no one in particular, but loud enough for Fran's ears.

"You will have two hours to prepare and cook your entry. Once the timer begins, you're in this room until you finish, for up to two hours. If you leave for any reason aside from a restroom break, you won't be allowed back in. If you need to use the restroom, someone from the Food Network will escort you."

"Those are pretty strict rules," said a balding man Fran didn't know by name.

"With ten thousand dollars at stake, what do you expect?" Corinne replied. "They want to make sure nobody cheats."

"That's right," Mark Todd said. "Winners in each of the five categories will be judged by a panel of five judges," he continued. "From those winners, one grand champion will be chosen to win the ten-thousand-dollar prize, along with an interview aired on Food Network and their recipe published by the Food Network. Questions?"

Fran knew the rules by heart. Apparently, so did everyone else, as no one spoke.

"Good thing you called Mitch," Joelle told Fran. "He saved your hide."

"If you ask me, he's done more than that to her hide." Noelle pointed at Fran's love bite and tittered.

Her face warm, Fran tugged up the neck of her sweater.

The sound of another buzzer filled the room. "Take your stations and start," Mark said. "The clock is ticking."

THREE HOURS LATER, a miracle had happened—Fran won the dessert category. Noelle and Joelle took the beverage category, but none of the other Friday Girls placed. That two contestants from their kitchen had won was very exciting.

After a hurried lunch from one of the festival booths, a sandwich Fran barely tasted, she, the twins and the three other category winners were seated in reserved front-row folding chairs of the packed Town Hall auditorium. Filling the seats around them were other contestants, locals, tourists and Food Network officials.

From time to time the busy Food Network cameras panned across Fran and the other winners, but after hours of filming, she was used to it and ignored them. Curt Blanco was here, too, snapping pictures for the next edition of the *Cranberry News Weekly*. Since he preferred what he called "natural poses" she ignored him, too.

The room hummed with conversation, but she heard none of it. What she focused on were the five Food Network judges, three females and two males, on stage. With sober expressions they studied the recipes provided by each category winner, sampled each of the five winning entries and scribbled notes on their scorecards.

The moment Fran had been working toward had at last arrived. Antsy and on edge, she shifted restlessly in the hard, uncomfortable chair. The judges seemed in no hurry, and the suspense was almost too much to bear.

Who would win? *Let them choose me.* Fran crossed her fingers on both hands. Then clenched them into fists. Then flexed.

Betsy, who had lost but wanted to lend her support,

sat directly behind her, knitting. She leaned forward. "You should have brought something to do while you wait. I have an extra pair of needles and yarn if you want them."

"Thanks, but I'm too nervous."

Noelle and Joelle, who sat on one side of Fran, seemed nervous, too. Every few minutes they squeezed each other's hands.

"I see Mitch," Joelle said, gesturing toward the side of the room. "Every time I glance at him he's looking at you."

Fran swiveled her head toward him. He gave a thumbs-up and flashed the grin that never failed to lift her heart.

"Just look at that smile on his handsome face." Noelle sighed. "What a man. You owe him big-time for bringing you those eggs. I hope you pay him back in a real special way, if you get my meaning."

"Don't you dare start up again," Joelle said, her voice louder. "Not here."

As tiresome as Noelle's suggestive comments and Joelle's disapproval were, at the moment, Fran didn't mind. Better to be distracted by the twins than stress out in silence.

"Be quiet, you two," Betsy whispered, pointing at the stage.

The judges were huddled together, their backs to the crowd. Stomach in knots, Fran fiddled with her braid, smoothed down her skirt, then laced her ice-cold fingers in her lap. Noelle and Joelle clasped hands again, and other finalists shifted in their seats.

As tension mounted the noise level in the room

dropped until silence filled the auditorium. Heart in her mouth, Fran glanced again at Mitch. He crossed his fingers and held them up.

At last, the judges beckoned to Mayor Eric Jannings, a portly male who ran Jannings Real Estate when he wasn't running Cranberry. They handed him a folded slip of paper.

With the cameras rolling and halogen lights flooding the stage, the mayor stepped to the microphone. He opened the paper. Shading his eyes against the brightness he squinted at it. Then nodded and smiled. "And now for the news you've all been waiting for. Third place overall goes to Noelle and Joelle Sommers in the drinks category, for their lover's cranberry soda with homemade cranberry-ginger ice cream."

Applause broke out. Wiping tears from their eyes the twins hurried on stage to accept a certificate and ribbon.

"Second place goes to Tim Hardy for his main-course category win—sweet and sour, candied cranberry meat loaf."

To more applause, a man Cinnamon didn't know climbed the stairs for his award.

Betsy squeezed Fran's shoulder. Noelle grabbed her hand. On pins and needles, Fran bit her lip and leaned forward.

"First place and grand champion for this year's cook-off, with an interview by Food Network, publication of the recipe and a check for ten thousand dollars, goes to Fran Bishop for her Out-Of-This-World, Blue-Ribbon Chocolate-Chunk Cranberry Bars."

Though Fran had hoped to win, hearing her name

was a shock. For a few seconds everything seemed to stand still. Then Betsy shoved her from behind.

"Go on up there and get your prize, champ."

Feeling oddly disconnected from herself, Fran climbed the stairs to the stage and moved toward the mayor. When she finally stood beside him and turned toward the audience, the lights were hot and so bright she couldn't see beyond the stage.

Beaming, Mayor Jannings handed her the check. They shook hands—hers cold, his warm. Then he hugged her. Teary-eyed, the win still not quite sinking in, she thanked him and the judges.

She posed as Curt snapped her picture for the paper, with the Food Network filming away. During the next half hour she never left the stage while fellow contestants, friends and acquaintances engulfed her in a flood of good wishes…including Mitch.

"Didn't I tell you?" Looking as pleased as she felt, he grinned. "I'm so proud of you."

Warmth and tenderness filled her. She loved him so much. She longed to rush into his arms and celebrate in a very private way. But that wasn't possible, not now.

"I couldn't have done it without your help," she said. "Thank you for being here, and for everything. And don't worry, I'm giving you credit."

"No need to. I was only teasing."

"Well, I'm not."

Smiling, he tucked a few stray strands of hair behind her ears.

"Ahem." Eyes twinkling, the mayor tapped her on the shoulder. "You're wanted at the judges' table."

Fran nodded. "I'm going to pitch my brunch cookbook to them," she murmured to Mitch.

"Good luck. I should get back to the Oceanside and work. You won't see me until breakfast tomorrow, but I want to hear everything then."

"Good luck, yourself."

She watched him walk away, then headed for the judges' table.

Chapter Fourteen

Five days after winning the cook-off, late Thursday morning, Fran and Betsy strolled around the Cranberry Festival booths in the field behind Town Hall, greeting friends, dodging throngs of people and enjoying the weak sunlight.

Since winning, Fran felt as if she'd been running nonstop, and welcomed the break. "I needed to relax like this," she said. "Thanks for dragging me away."

"Anytime, but I have ulterior motives. I've never wandered the Cranberry Festival with a grand champion." Betsy grinned. "Have you come down from the clouds yet?"

"Not yet." Laughing, Fran shook her head. "I keep thinking I'll wake up and find out this has all been a dream. A wonderful, very busy dream."

Between attention from winning the cook-off, caring for her guests, helping with Cranberry Festival events and several visits to Cinnamon and Nick's, she barely had time to think. The days had flown by in a blur.

"What's going on with the brunch cookbook?"

"The Food Network people want to see it before

Christmas. That they're interested at all is another miracle." Fran shook her head in amazement. "I'm fine-tuning and testing some of the recipes on my guests."

"I'll bet they like that."

"So far. There's the arts-and-crafts tent." Fran nodded toward the giant yellow-and-white-striped tent straight ahead. "I haven't had time to stop in there yet. Let's go support our local artists and buy something."

While they browsed through booth after booth in the heated tent, Fran thought about Mitch. He'd like some of this stuff, but he was working twenty hours a day to finish the book and couldn't get away.

Except for breakfast. That was the highlight of her day, when she saw him—exhausted, but his old, warm self. Her guests adored him, and so did she.

Once or twice, after everyone had left the table for walks on the beach or a trip to the Cranberry Festival, Mitch had pulled her close for dizzying kisses. She sighed happily. What a man.

Remembering that he'd wanted to buy one of Foster Gravis's pieces, she headed for his booth, while Betsy studied hand-stitched doll clothes several booths over.

Foster, who sat on a stool behind a table filled with his creations, grinned at her. "Hello there, Fran. Congratulations on your win. You look radiant this morning."

"I'm very happy. Thanks."

"How's Mitch's book coming along?"

"He told you about that?"

"You'd be surprised at the things we've discussed."

Wasn't that curious? Well, Mitch had said they were friends. "The writing's going really well, but he's barely taking the time to eat and sleep."

A young couple stopped to buy something, and Foster left Fran to look over his creations. There were dozens of carvings done in several kinds of wood, each artfully mounted on driftwood. Was this the driftwood Mitch had helped Foster gather the day they'd met?

When Foster finished with his customers, he turned to Fran. "You're still here."

"I want to buy a piece for Mitch," she said.

"What strikes your fancy?"

She pointed to a charming carving of a seagull in flight, held above the driftwood by a stick. "Is that your only seagull?"

"The last one left."

"He reminds me of Stumpy, one of the gulls I feed. Mitch would like it, I think. I'll take it."

"Well, now, isn't that interesting."

Foster chuckled, as if she'd said something funny. Fran gave a mental shrug. She paid him, and he carefully wrapped the work in newspaper.

"Give him my regards," Foster said.

"I certainly will."

She would wait to give him the gull until he finished the book. She imagined his pleased grin. Maybe they'd sneak into the garage and he'd pull her close and kiss her until they both were breathless with need....

Fran almost groaned at the thought. She could hardly wait until everyone checked out on Sunday, and had no doubt that, once the door closed behind the last person, she and Mitch would fall into each other's arms and stay that way until Tuesday morning—one long love-fest before he left town.

After that… Her heart surely would break with missing him. But she was used to being alone. She'd survive.

She joined Betsy, who shot her a puzzled look. "Whatever you bought certainly sobered your mood."

"This is a Foster Gravis wood carving. I'm just coming down after being so busy. Speaking of busy…I hate to say this, but I should get back."

"Such is the life of the grand-champion cook-off winner." Betsy grinned. "My shop opens at noon, so I can't stay much longer, either. On the way out, let's stop at the scone booth." She lowered her voice. "It's that time of month and I always crave bread."

That time of the month. With so much happening, Fran hadn't given a thought to her cycle. Her period should've started Sunday. She was late.

She'd always been regular, her cycle exactly twenty-seven days long. Only once had she been late—eight years ago.

No. She couldn't be pregnant. Surely she'd miscalculated.

Betsy bought herself a scone, and they walked slowly toward their cars, Fran somehow managing to put on a happy face. The second she drove out of the parking lot, she sobered and raced home, her mind whirling.

HANDS SHAKING, Fran let herself into her basement apartment. Rushing into the bedroom, she dug into the drawer of her bedside table, where she stored the calendar her mother had taught her to keep. There she dutifully recorded the first day of every cycle.

Unfortunately, there was no mistake. She truly was late. *Dear God.* The past came rushing back, along with the same tumultuous emotions—confusion, fear and excitement. Incredulous, Fran sank onto her bed. She stared at the grand-champion ribbon on the dresser without really seeing it. What to do, what to do…

First off, she needed a pregnancy test. She'd buy a kit from the drugstore. Right now.

Grateful that Mitch was upstairs working and everyone else was out, she stood and shrugged into her coat. Seconds later she was in her car, backing out of the garage.

Because she knew everyone at the local drugstore, she drove to the next town over. The pregnancy-test kit she chose claimed ninety-seven percent accuracy.

Locked in a drafty gas station bathroom she took the test. Waiting three full minutes in the dirty facility seemed like forever, but, at the same time, not nearly long enough. The same as eight years ago, only then she'd lived in Portland and had taken the test in her apartment. But her terror and pounding heart was the same.

When at last she screwed up her courage and checked the test strip, two solid pink lines greeted her, confirming what she already knew. She was, indeed, pregnant.

Numb, she made her way to the car. She wasn't ready for a baby, especially when the father-to-be wasn't in love with her. Yet, despite the shock, she was thrilled. A baby of her own! *What if I miscarry?* She pushed that awful thought away. Her doctor at the time had assured her that many women miscarry the first time and that he saw no reason why she wouldn't have a full-term, healthy baby if she tried again.

On the drive back to Cranberry, vacillating between joy and dread—a baby!—she debated what to do next.

A doctor's appointment to confirm the results was a must. Before that though, she ought to tell Mitch.

The very thought worried her. He wouldn't be happy about this—might even be angry, probably at himself.

News as unexpected as this could interfere with his writing. Fran couldn't let that happen. She would wait until he finished the book. Or maybe she wouldn't tell him at all… A few more days and he'd be gone.

But that was a coward's way out and wasn't fair to him. This was his baby, too, and he deserved to know.

She would tell him, only, not just yet.

AT FOUR O'CLOCK Friday morning Mitch typed *The End* on the computer screen. He'd done it, finished the book. Drained, relieved and euphoric, he sent e-mails to his agent and editor, promising the polished version next week, then yawned and closed his laptop.

He couldn't wait to tell Fran. With a house full of guests to cook for, she wouldn't sleep past five. He would shower, sneak downstairs and share the good news. And maybe convince her to stay in bed awhile longer for a private celebration. His blood warmed in anticipation. They both had things to celebrate—the book and her contest win.

Trouble was, she didn't want him in her bed until everyone checked out. But Mitch couldn't wait any longer. And, with no one else awake yet, where was the harm? For good luck, he'd bring the seagull wood carving and give it to her now, as a late congratulatory gift.

Twenty minutes later, shaved, showered, dressed and eager for her, holding the carving, he stood in the dark threshold of her apartment and knocked softly on the door.

She opened it wearing a yellow terry cloth robe, her face scrubbed and her wet hair combed and streaming down her back. He drank in the sight.

"Mitch," she whispered with wide eyes. "What are you doing awake at this hour?"

A table lamp lit the burgundy oriental rug, dark bookcase and beige sofa. Beyond, the bedroom and bathroom lights were on. With her robe pulled tight he could only see a sliver of skin at her throat, but that was enough to fuel his hunger.

Wishing he'd shown up in time to shower with her, wondering if she were naked under the robe, he let his gaze travel slowly over her, stopping at her gold-colored toenails. "I worked all night and just finished the book. I couldn't wait to tell you. Brought you a gift, too, a late congrats for your win. Gonna let me in?"

The door widened. "That's wonderful about the book. And thanks for the beautiful carving." She hardly glanced at it, didn't even look pleased to see him. Just nibbled her lower lip.

Was she that worried about her guests? Mitch closed the door as quietly as possible. "At this hour it's a sure bet that everyone else is asleep. I swear, I'll be gone before anyone wakes up. That's a Foster Gravis."

"Yes."

"The two gulls remind me of Stubby and Stumpy," he said.

"You're right, they do." She set the art on the coffee table. "Funny, I bought you a Foster Gravis carving, too, for when you finished the book. No wonder Foster laughed. Wait here and I'll get it."

In seconds, she was back with a newspaper-wrapped package.

Mitch tore off the paper. "A seagull. We got each other the same thing. How cool is that? Guess that means we think alike. Thanks." He grinned, but Fran did not.

Well, she hadn't had her morning coffee. Intending to study the work later and wanting to thank her in a more intimate way, he set his gift on the bookshelf beside the door, then reached for her.

Instead of walking into his arms she averted her head. "Don't."

Surprised and hurt, he dropped his hands. "I thought you'd be happy for me, that you'd want to celebrate."

"I am happy for you, Mitch."

If she bit her lip any more she'd chew it right off. And why wouldn't she look at him? For the first time, he noted the shadows under her eyes and her unusually pale skin.

"Are you sick?" he asked, worried.

She shook her head. "We need to talk, but there isn't time just now. I have to blow-dry my hair, start the yeast rolls and cut up fruit for the honeyed fruit salad. And you need sleep."

We need to talk meant only one thing. Now she had him scared. Mitch narrowed his eyes. "If you're dumping me, just say it."

"You know I'm not."

The startled expression on her face told him that was true. "Then, what is it?"

She held his gaze, as if gauging whether to answer the question, looked away and released a heavy sigh. "All right, we'll talk now. But you're not going to like this."

She gestured for him to take a seat, choosing an oak rocking chair for herself.

With curiosity and foreboding Mitch turned the adjacent armchair to face her and sat down.

Hugging her waist, she pushed the rocker with her foot, her face as solemn as a clergyperson at a funeral.

God knew what she was about to say. Silence filled the air, broken only by the creak of the chair. With a sense of dread, Mitch waited.

At last, she looked at him. "I'm pregnant."

The words took a moment to penetrate. "Pregnant," he repeated, frowning. He'd never expected this. "Are you sure?"

"I took the test yesterday. I'm sure."

"Those things aren't always reliable."

"This one claimed ninety-seven percent accuracy."

His arguments neatly refuted, he could only give his head a stunned shake. "You said you were safe."

"Obviously I was wrong."

He scrubbed both hands over his face, shaved smooth for her.

"Is that all you have to say?"

She sounded angry. He looked at her, but couldn't read her face. "You just dropped a bomb on me, Fran. Give me a minute to process it."

Nodding, she tugged wet strands of hair. The rocker continued its rhythmic creak.

Mitch imagined her in the same chair, cradling a newborn in arms. His kid.

A baby. Holy cow.

He wasn't ready for this. Lately, he barely could hold himself together, let alone take on this new burden.

Elbows on his thighs, head in his hands, he stared at the carpet.

Hadn't his father schooled him to maintain control at all times? He'd let go, and look what had happened?

He blew out a loud breath and raised his gaze. "What do you want to do?"

The rocking stopped. Fran's chin lifted. She looked straight at him. "Keep her."

No surprise there. His back was against a wall and there was only one thing to do. "Then we should get married."

She shook her head. "I don't want to marry you."

Now *that* surprised him. "Why the hell not?"

"I've been down this path before, Mitch. You only asked out of a sense of duty, and that's not enough." She gave a sad smile. "You'd always resent me, and I couldn't bear that. And if…" She captured a lock of hair and frowned at the ends. "If anything happened to the baby, you'd walk out and *I'd* end up resenting *you*. I'd rather stay as we are. Friends."

Mitch refused to listen. He'd been raised to accept responsibility for his actions, and wasn't about to walk away. "I'm not like the bum you were engaged to," he said, wondering if maybe he was. "You're pregnant with my baby. We're getting married."

Fran rolled her eyes. "This isn't the dark ages, Mitch. Single women have and raise kids all the time."

"Not my kid." He clamped his jaw and eyed her.

Her own jaw set. "Look, you're welcome to be a part of our child's life, and I'll gladly accept child support." She crossed her arms. "But I will not marry you."

He'd never seen this stubborn side of her. Galled, he

glared at her. "Dammit, Fran!" He pounded the arm of his chair. "That's just plain crazy."

His intimidating look and voice didn't even phase her. "If that's they way you see it, fine. But I've made up my mind." She stood. "Now, it's getting late and I really should dress and start breakfast."

He'd lost this round, but, after he slept and did more thinking, he was sure he'd be able to persuade her to do the right thing and marry him. He, too, stood. "We'll finish this conversation later."

"There's nothing more to say." She nodded at the bookshelf, where he'd set her gift to him. Then pulling herself up tall, she opened the door and waited for him to go.

No more to say? The hell there wasn't. His temper again flared. Only with supreme effort did he hold it in check. There was no way he could pretend life was good and make small talk this morning. He snatched his wood carving from the shelf.

"I'm going upstairs to get some sleep, so I won't be at breakfast," he said, cursing the damned guests. "But, when I wake up, I'll find you and we *will* talk."

IN THE YEARS since Fran had owned and run the Oceanside she'd always enjoyed taking care of her guests. But, today, she wished they'd go away.

"Where's Mitch this morning?" Nina asked.

Fran didn't want to talk about Mitch, or think about him. She'd never seen him angry until this morning. Quite intimidating, but nothing he said or did would change her mind. If he thought he could persuade her to marry him with narrowed eyes and loud words, he was wrong.

She only would consider marriage if he loved her. And he didn't.

"Um, he's probably sleeping in." Pasting a cheerful smile on her face, she brought the coffeepot into the dining room. "More coffee, anyone?"

As she refilled mugs, Patty O'Callahan frowned. "But he paid for breakfast and he's been here every morning. There are only two more chances to enjoy your cooking before we all check out. Maybe he's sick or something."

"A man's entitled to sleep late if he wants," Bryan added. "He probably partied last night, or worked on that project he mentioned. Right, Fran?"

"I'm not sure," she lied. "This is the last weekend before the Cranberry Festival ends, and the festival organizers have planned some wonderful activities. And, while you're eating, please think about the frittata. I'd really like your input for the cookbook."

The talk turned to things to do in Cranberry and the food, and the rest of the meal passed smoothly, without another word about Mitch.

By the time Fran jotted down notes about the frittata and cleaned up the kitchen, everyone had gone out.

Alone at last, except for Mitch, who was sleeping. She let out a relieved sigh and started to pour herself a cup of coffee—then stopped. Caffeine wasn't good for the baby. She brewed a cup of herbal tea and sat down with a magazine.

The house was way too quiet. How would she bear the silence when everyone left, when Mitch went away? At least he hadn't lied and pretended he loved her. She was grateful for his honesty.

She gave up on the magazine, slipped her favorite Norah Jones CD into the disc player, pulled out the frittata recipe and incorporated her notes. The heartfelt song only made her feel lonely. She tried a different, more lighthearted track, but despite the upbeat music her spirits plunged.

She shut it off and called Doc Bartlett, Cranberry's only family-practice doctor. The other doctors had moved to a clinic outside town, but he'd kept his office downtown. Saying she needed a checkup—no sense alerting the receptionist to the real reason—she scheduled an appointment. The doctor was booked until the second week of November, a week and a half from now.

Too antsy to stay home, Fran decided to run errands. Not that there were any this morning. Well, she'd figure out something. A new paperback book or something from the library would do.

As she shrugged into her coat she thought about visiting Cinnamon and Callie instead, but the baby kept Cinnamon too busy for a heart-to-heart. And Nick would be there, with them. Cinnamon, Callie and Nick—a real family.

Fran's throat clogged up and tears stung the backs of her eyes. She couldn't risk crying in front of Cinnamon, who would ask questions. Fran wasn't ready to share her secret just yet, not until after Doc Bartlett confirmed the pregnancy.

Until then, no one but Mitch would know.

Chapter Fifteen

Mitch woke from a dreamless sleep, rested and starved. The clock and the gathering darkness told him he'd slept twelve hours. He'd finished the book. Elated, he folded his hands behind his head and grinned—for all of two seconds.

Then he remembered. Fran was pregnant with his baby. And she wouldn't marry him. Swearing, he swung his legs over the bed, then stalked into the bathroom.

Standing under the hot spray of the shower, he recalled her words and that stubborn tilt of her chin. *You only asked out of a sense of duty, and that's no way to start a marriage. You'd always resent me.*

She was right—the thought of marrying Fran had not crossed his mind until he found out she was pregnant. But outside the reason for the proposal he wasn't like the twerp she was engaged to before. Mitch enjoyed her company, loved talking and laughing with her. The sex was great, too, and she was a fantastic cook. Best of all, he trusted her.

In his mind, not a bad way to start a marriage. The more he thought about it, the better he liked the idea.

He would talk to Fran again, right away. Using reasoning and common sense, surely he'd convince her that marriage was their best option.

As he toweled dry, his stomach growled. He hadn't eaten in twenty-four hours. Best grab something from the fridge, first. Then find Fran.

THE FINAL wine-and-cheese social of the tourist season was over. All the guests had gone out to enjoy dinner and wander through the shops that were still open—one last, enjoyable evening in Cranberry. Followed by one more brunch in the morning.

Fran straightened the kitchen with less than her usual energy. Today had been an emotional roller coaster, her feelings fluctuating from panic to excitement to worry to joy and back again.

At the moment, as she tossed empty wine bottles into the recycle bin outside the back door, she felt a quiet certainty that she could do this by herself, raise her baby right here at the Oceanside.

She wasn't really alone. Back inside, she swiped crumbs from the counter into her hand. There were so many friends who would willingly help. With their support and Mitch's financial assistance, she and the baby would manage quite well.

It was a shame that Mitch lived a long way from here. He was a busy man, and Fran doubted the baby would see much of her father. Both father and child would lose out, which was sad.

But who wanted a man to marry her out of obligation?

As she pulled out clean place mats for tomorrow's breakfast, footsteps thudded across the entry.

No need to guess who that was. Mitch. Awake at last.

For the first time in ages, Fran's heart filled with apprehension instead of anticipation. She dreaded another confrontation. Stifling the urge to flee, she positioned the place mats around the dining room table.

"Hello, Fran."

He looked rested and heart-stoppingly handsome. The man she loved. But, if he started his macho marry-me talk, she'd walk away.

"You slept a long time," she said, moving into the kitchen. Away from him. "I'll bet you're hungry."

He nodded and followed her. "Thought I'd make myself a sandwich. If that's okay with you."

Only yesterday, she'd enjoyed having him in her kitchen. Now the room felt much too crowded. "I'll make it for you."

"You should be sitting down."

Resisting the urge to roll her eyes, she shook her head. "I'm fine, Mitch. Why don't you sit down, instead? Ham or roast beef?"

"Roast beef," he said, grabbing a glass from the cabinet.

She opened the refrigerator and pulled out the water pitcher. Then the bread and sandwich fixings.

After pouring himself a glass of water, he sat at the kitchen table, giving her space at last. Fran heaved a relieved breath, turned her back and put the sandwich together.

Even though she couldn't see him she felt his gaze. She wished he'd stop staring, wished he'd say something to break the oddly full silence. But he didn't, so she did.

"You slept through a beautiful autumn day. The sun

was out all afternoon. What a perfect way to wind down the Cranberry Festival."

"Sorry I missed that."

As she set the sandwich and a handful of carrot sticks on a plate in front of him, he clasped her wrist.

"Sit with me?"

"Um, I can't." She pulled out of his grasp. "I have things to do downstairs." The statement wasn't true, but she needed some excuse.

"Don't make me eat alone."

Who could resist that pleading look? Reluctantly, she nodded, pulling plates from the cabinet and laying them on the place mats rather than joining him at the table. He ate quickly, like a man on the edge of starvation and, by the time he finished, the table was set for breakfast.

"Would you like anything else?" she asked.

"Yeah. To talk." He pushed aside his plate. "Why don't you sit down here, with me. I swear, I won't bite."

No, but he sure as heck could persuade. Or try. Bracing for what was to come, she sat at one end of the small table. "All right, but I won't change my mind."

Under the table she felt the warmth of his legs and knew their knees were almost touching.

"A baby needs a mother and a father. That's a darned good reason for us to get married."

Fran sighed and rested her head on her fist. "We already had this conversation. She'll have us both, just not in the same house." Or in the same town. "You can see her whenever you want."

"You mean, joint custody."

She hadn't thought of that, didn't really like the idea,

but it was only fair. "If that's what you want, but with us living so far apart, that'll be hard on her."

"Then, let's make it easy." Reaching across the space between them he caught her hands in his. "We're good together, Fran."

It was true. She pulled free and stared at a scratch on the table.

He tipped up her chin, his fingers warm and solid. "Would marriage to me be so bad?"

His dark, searching gaze touched her heart and weakened her resolve. God help her, she wanted to marry him. But he didn't love her, and there was a baby to think of.

She leaned back, away from his grasp. "Did you not hear a word I said this morning? I don't want marriage without love."

"There's nothing I can do to change your mind, is there?"

"No."

His eyes glittered and narrowed. "You're a damned stubborn woman."

"I am when I know I'm right." Trembling for some reason, Fran stood. "And I'd appreciate it if you respected my decision."

Exhaling loudly, Mitch threw up his hands. "Suit yourself."

"Thank you." She locked her hands at her waist. "It'll be easier on both of us if you leave in the morning."

"You really want that?"

What she wanted was Mitch's love. "I really do."

He gave a terse nod and stood. "I'll be out of here before breakfast. But this isn't over."

BEFORE DAWN Saturday morning, Mitch brought down his bags, laptop and the seagull wood carving—the crude bowl he had made was tucked into a suitcase—and set them beside the front door. He hadn't slept worth a damn, but Fran wanted him gone, and he would go. Unless she'd changed her mind....

He found her in the kitchen, making coffee and starting breakfast. "'Morning."

"Good morning."

There were sleep shadows under her eyes, and he knew she hadn't slept well, either. He moved toward her. Though she wouldn't meet his gaze she didn't back away.

Filled with expectation, he caressed her cheek. "If you want, I'll stay."

She turned away. "Please, Mitch. Just go."

"All right."

He paid his bill. Neither of them spoke as Fran accompanied him to the door.

"Call if you need anything," he said.

She nodded.

Until the last second he hoped she'd surprise them both and ask him to stay. But she opened the door without a word, and he walked outside.

"I'll be in touch," he said.

The door closed behind him, the latch clicking and final. With a heavy heart, he hefted his belongings and walked toward his car.

TEN DAYS AFTER returning to Seattle, after working long hours to polish his book, Mitch sent the final version overnight delivery to Kathryn. She read it within twenty-four hours and called to sing his praises, then forwarded copies to Sylvia and Peter Jakes. Both were equally pleased.

Kathryn and Sylvia reminded him that it was the right time to expand the business worldwide. Signings. Speaking tours. Maybe merchandising. He hadn't made up his mind yet, but promised to make a decision soon.

For all the pain of writing, the book had turned out well. Mitch should have been euphoric. Instead, he felt empty, almost as bad as when he'd first arrived at the Oceanside.

This time though, he understood why. Fran wasn't here to celebrate with him. They hadn't spoken since the Saturday morning he'd driven away. Oh, he'd tried, had called often. But she didn't pick up, and never called back, even though he left voice mail and e-mail messages asking her to.

Either she'd left town for a while or she didn't want to talk to him. Since she hadn't mentioned going anyplace, he figured it was the latter.

Stubborn woman. If he could just talk to her again, he would tell her what she meant to him. At eight o'clock on a Tuesday, she ought to be home. Sitting at his table, he glanced around his state-of-the-art, stainless-steel kitchen. So cold and sterile compared to Fran's colorful, warm rooms.

Damn, but he missed her. He used the landline, which would come up as "private caller" on her caller ID. After seven rings, her voice mail clicked on.

"It's Mitch," he said. "I was hoping you'd answer tonight. There are things I want to know. How you're doing, have you seen the doctor, what's going on with the cookbook?" He was rambling now, but once he'd started, it was hard to stop. "But I guess you don't want to talk to me. I sent off the book. It's my best yet, and I dedicated it to you."

If she was home and listening, maybe now she'd pick up. Only, she didn't. Mitch cleared his throat. "I'll hang up now. If I don't hear from you soon, I'll try again. Good night, and sleep well."

He moved to the living room and dropped onto the sofa. Foster's wood carving, the gull Fran had given him, sat prominently on the coffee table in front of him. Mitch thought about the old man and his valuable life lessons. As promised, he'd bought himself a set of tools but hadn't used them yet.

Once again, his life was out of balance. He retrieved the ugly bowl he'd made, which he'd stowed in the coat closet, and took out his tools. What had Foster said? *Feel what's below the surface of the wood. If you like what you feel, rework the piece.*

Mitch liked this piece of wood. He would rework it until he was satisfied. He started to work, his thoughts on Fran. Once finished, the bowl would be hers.

Several hours later, pleased with this new, improved bowl, he turned in, leaving wood shavings all over the gleaming hardwood floors of his living room. Although he'd been up early and it was almost eleven, he tossed and turned, missing Fran so much, he ached. Could they rework their relationship as he had the bowl?

Lying in the darkness, he composed what he would say to her when they did talk. Because, sooner or later, she'd have to answer the phone. Only, instead of imagining a phone conversation, he fantasized that she was lying beside him.

"Do you have any idea how important you are to me?" he said, staring into the blackness. In his imagination the reading light was on and they were lying on their sides, facing each other. "Your generosity and friendship have filled up the emptiness."

He pictured her expression, softening and warming with each word. Eyes glowing, lips curling into that special smile that made him feel valued and important. He would thread her fingers in his and kiss each knuckle. When her eyelids drifted shut he would kiss them, then take her mouth deeply and honestly, holding back nothing.

If he were lucky, she'd share her passion with him. He would lose himself in it, in her.

Caught up in the fantasy, his body taut and throbbing, he groaned. "I love you, Fran."

Words that had never before passed his lips.

They hung in the air, stunning him.

He loved Fran. Profoundly and completely.

His chest full, he sat up in bed. Switched on the bedside lamp, blinked and shook his head.

What a blind fool he'd been. How had he ever considered a life without Fran—without love? Talk about a thick-skulled bozo. He added half a dozen other derogatory names before he swore he heard his father laughing and shut his mouth.

Then, plain as the sailboat painting on the wall, he heard his father's voice. *Don't sit around cursing yourself, boy. Do something about it.*

"I will, Dad," he uttered softly. "Thanks for the advice

about marriage. I think I finally understand. You and Foster were talking about the same thing—balance."

Eager to take action, Mitch went to his office, woke up the computer and sent a quick e-mail to Peter Jakes, asking him to add *I love you, Fran* to the dedication.

He couldn't wait to tell Fran—in person, so that he could hold her and show her the depths of his love. He thought about kissing her belly where their baby was growing and laughed out loud for sheer joy.

This was what happiness felt like. He picked up his cell to tell her he was on his way. But it was after eleven and she was probably in bed. She likely wouldn't answer, anyway.

Too late to call, but not to hit the road. Driving all night, he'd get there first thing in the morning. He threw his clothes into a suitcase, grabbed the bowl, jumped into his car and sped off.

Chapter Sixteen

Even a week and a half after her guests left, Fran hadn't adjusted to the peace and quiet. Tuesday night she soaked in the bathtub in her apartment, surrounded by candles, with a jazz fusion CD to keep her company.

Evenings were hard, but the days weren't nearly as lonely. She filled the time by thoroughly cleaning every nook and cranny in the Oceanside, working on the brunch cookbook and visiting friends. Especially Cinnamon, Nick and Callie.

The warmth in their home was a balm to her broken heart, and if she couldn't have her own loving family, she would be a part of theirs. Later, her child would, too.

"You're going to love the Mahoney family," she told the life growing inside her. Recently, she'd read that talking to your baby was good, and had gotten into the habit of voicing her most positive thoughts.

With love and tenderness, she washed her still-flat belly. "We're going to see Doc Bartlett tomorrow morning. He looks like Santa Claus, but he's a good doctor."

Cinnamon knew about Mitch, but not the pregnancy,

and keeping the secret had been difficult. But, once the doctor confirmed what Fran already knew… "Then I can tell everyone I know about you. Won't Cinnamon be thrilled?"

Of course, with Mitch not here to share in the celebration… Fran missed him terribly, but, though he'd e-mailed and left numerous voice messages, she couldn't summon up the strength to call him back. Not without falling apart. Pregnancy hormones and a broken heart did that to a woman. Anyway, what was the point? They'd already discussed everything. Maybe later, when she had a better grip on her feelings.

And she'd sat here long enough. She opened the drain and stood. "We're going to be fine," she assured the baby—and herself.

As she padded out of the bathroom in her pajamas and slippers, she heard Mitch's voice. "I'll hang up now. If I don't hear from you soon, I'll try again. Good night, and sleep well."

Her heart yearning and sore, she replayed the message, tearing up when she heard about the dedication. He sounded as if he genuinely missed her. Even though he may not love her, he was suffering, too. She glanced at the seagull wood carving he'd given her. "We think alike," he'd said, when he'd unwrapped her gift to him.

The carving and his call tonight made her feel close to him. She decided she wanted to talk, after all, but was too tired to call now. She'd phone him tomorrow, after the doctor's appointment.

In the middle of the night a familiar ache started low in her belly, waking her from a deep sleep. It felt as if…as if her monthly were about to start.

The miscarriage eight years ago had started this same way. Terrified, she switched on the light. "Please, please, please," she whispered into the empty silence.

She ought to go into the bathroom and check for blood. But she was too scared. *Oh, Mitch.* It was three-thirty in the morning. He'd be asleep. She hadn't returned any of his calls. She might cry. None of that mattered now. He should know about this. More important, she needed him.

Clutching the phone she called. First the landline, then his cell. He didn't answer. After leaving messages on both, she curled into a ball and prayed.

DAYLIGHT WAS JUST penetrating the cloud-laden sky when Mitch drove up Fran's driveway.

Save for the motion-sensitive outdoor lights, the house was dark. At just after seven she was asleep. As eager as Mitch was to see her, she and the baby she was carrying needed their rest. He backed out, drove to the fast-food place on the outskirts of town, ate breakfast, shaved with his electric razor and cleaned up. Just after eight he returned to Fran's.

To his surprise the lights were still off.

She never slept this late. Maybe she *was* out of town. Mitch didn't know that he could handle that. After nine-plus hours of thinking and driving he was psyched to tell her how he felt—right now.

He exited the car and peered through the window in the garage. To his relief, her car was there. Sleeping or not, he couldn't wait one more second. The front door to her apartment faced the driveway. He strode to it and knocked.

Moments later the chain on the door rattled. "Who is it?" she asked, her voice muffled through the door.

"Mitch."

The door clicked and opened. She was still in her pajamas, her hair tangled and falling down her back. Her nose and eyes were red and swollen and her skin was pale.

To him, she looked beautiful. But maybe she'd caught the flu. He took hold of her hands—her cold hands. "Are you sick?"

Biting her lip she shook her head. "I can't believe you're here." Tears filled her eyes. "I've been trying to call you for hours."

"You have?" Music to his ears. Having read that a pregnant woman's hormones often caused an intense show of feelings, he wasn't alarmed. "I turned off my cell. Everything will be all right now."

Not about to let go of her now that he at last was touching her, he grasped her arm, keeping her close while he shut the door. "You have no idea how much I've missed you."

"Oh, Mitch." Her face crumpled and new tears spilled from her eyes. "How did you know?"

Know what? Catching hold of her hand he led her to the sofa. She sank down as if her legs couldn't hold her.

He joined her. "I have something important to say."

"Can it wait?" Her chin trembled. "I'm afraid I might be losing the b-baby." Sobs racked her body.

"What?" Sick at heart, he tucked her hair behind her ears and held her. "How do you know? Have you called the doctor? Maybe you're fine."

"I've had cramps and some s-spotting." Sniffling,

she pulled a tissue from the box on the end table and wiped her eyes. "I have an appointment at the doctor's at nine. Will you drive me?"

"Of course. Do you need help getting dressed?"

She shook her head. "I can do it. Just please, don't leave me."

"Never again. I'll be right here on the sofa, waiting for you."

Mitch hoped she was wrong. Scared, his chest hurting for Fran and their baby, he waited. The minutes dragged by like weeks. He heard her pad into the bathroom, then the sound of the water. Ordinary sounds now weighted with anguish.

The words he needed to say—that he wanted to marry her, not out of a sense of duty, but because he loved her—seemed more important than ever, but they would have to wait.

Finally she stood before him, ashen and scared. "I'm ready now."

Mitch wished he could ease her fears, but there was nothing he could do. He helped her into her coat and they headed for the doctor's office.

FRAN TRUDGED into Doc Bartlett's bright waiting room leaning into Mitch, his strength keeping her from falling apart. She wondered why he'd shown up now and what he meant by "something important to say." Whatever it was, she needed him more than she ever needed anyone.

Audrey Eames, the plump, fiftysomething receptionist-nurse behind the check-in station, looked from Mitch to Fran with wide eyes. "Land sakes, Fran. Are you all right?"

Having skipped her usual makeup and barely run a comb through her hair, she knew she must look awful. She also knew that if she tried to speak, she'd cry.

"Fran has a nine o'clock appointment with the doctor," Mitch said. "She needs to see him now and she needs to sit down. Is there an exam room available?"

Audrey squinted at Mitch. "Just who are you?"

"Mitch Matthews. I'm in love with Fran."

Had she heard right? Fran looked up at him. His eyes were filled with assurance and feeling.

Mitch loved her. For a moment, her world brightened and her heart swelled with warmth.

Did you hear that, baby? Your daddy loves me, and I know he loves you. So please, stay and grow strong. Please.

He kissed her forehead and shifted her closer to his side.

"Well, isn't that something?" Audrey grinned before she sobered again. "I can put you in room four. Follow me." She left her desk and headed through the crowded waiting room.

Fran noted familiar faces, all of them no doubt having heard everything. Smiles greeted her, muted with concern, and she knew that they wondered what was wrong.

Terrified, she managed to nod, then followed Audrey. In the small room, Mitch hung up her slacks and panties, helped her onto the exam table and handed her the paper cover. She draped it over herself and waited for Doc, with Mitch standing beside her, clasping her hand.

"What you said to Audrey? Did you mean that, Mitch?" she asked, holding her breath.

"That I love you? I sure did. I do. I drove all night to

tell you." He stroked her cheek. "This isn't exactly how I pictured telling you. I had a speech ready and meant to kneel at your feet when I proposed. Marry me, Fran. Not out of obligation, but because I can't imagine life without you."

This was what Fran had longed for and dreamed of. But now... She bit her lip. "What if I lose the baby?"

Profound sorrow filled his face, and he swallowed hard. "That'd hurt like hell. But pregnant or not, I want to spend the rest of my life with you."

"Oh, Mitch, I love you, too. Yes, I'll marry you."

As he bent down to kiss her a sharp rap sounded. The doctor entered the room. Mitch straightened, but not before the portly man's gray eyes flashed behind his gold-rimmed bifocals.

"Hello, Fran," he said through his neatly trimmed, snow-white beard.

"This is Mitch Matthews," she said. "My fiancé. Meet Doc."

They shook hands.

"What seems to be the problem?" the doctor asked.

Anxiety flooded back, but Mitch's hand on her shoulder steadied her.

"I'm pregnant and I think I'm losing the baby."

The doctor pulled off his latex gloves. "Everything feels normal. You're still pregnant."

Standing near her head, Mitch exhaled loudly while Doc Bartlett tossed the gloves into a covered trash receptacle, then washed his hands.

Daring to hope, her lower body hidden by the paper cover, Fran sat up and eyed the man. "You're sure?"

Not used to being questioned, he frowned and stroked his beard. "I've been treating pregnant women for forty years now, so I should know."

Fran glanced at her lap. "Yes, but I miscarried about eight years ago." In silent support, Mitch squeezed her shoulder, and she gratefully absorbed his strength. "I'm scared."

"That was a long time ago, Fran. You're a healthy woman, doing fine. About three weeks along."

"Thank God." The heaviness that had weighted her down since the middle of the night melted away. She smiled at Mitch. "We're having a baby. I can't believe it."

Water flooded his eyes. "Thanks, doctor."

"What about the cramping and the spotting?" she asked.

"Perfectly normal those first few months. Now, if the cramping gets worse or the spotting increases, you'll want to come back. You'll come back, anyway, next month for a checkup—schedule that with Audrey before you leave."

"Should I cut back on any activities?"

"I wouldn't drink alcohol or caffeine and I suggest you pick up some prenatal vitamins. Otherwise, go about your life."

"What about sex, Doc?" Mitch asked. "Not today, but when she's feeling better?"

Fran's cheeks warmed, but she was glad Mitch had asked.

"Absolutely fine." Without a trace of embarrassment, Doc Bartlett manipulated a cardboard wheel that looked as if it had been around since he'd opened his practice. "How does the sixth of July sound? That's your probable due date."

As happy as Fran was, she groaned. "Right in the middle of tourist season?"

"Don't worry," Mitch said. "I'll be here to help."

She couldn't quite picture him pampering her guests. She touched his smooth face and realized that, even though he'd driven all night, he'd shaved for her. "You don't have to, Mitch. Seattle's your home and—"

"I can see I'm no longer wanted here," Doc Bartlett said with a smile. "Leave the door open when you go." He slipped out and closed the door behind him.

"I don't want to give up the Oceanside," Fran continued. "But, if you want to live in Seattle, I will."

Mitch joined her on the exam table, his thigh flush and warm against hers. "I'd never ask you to do that. I can work anyplace. On the drive down I did some thinking. I'd like to rent a space in town and start a training facility to train others. Kathryn and Sylvia want me to take my business worldwide. I figure I'll let the people I hire do that for me. That way I can spend most of my time here with you."

"You'd do that for me?"

"It's called 'balance.'" He gave her a tender smile. "I'm hoping you'll come on my book tour with me—if you're not too pregnant."

That sounded fun. "I'll come," Fran said.

"Anything else?"

"Only that I love you, Mitch Matthews."

"Love you, too." Mitch kissed her gently.

Filled with warmth and joy, Fran kissed him back. When Mitch released her, she sighed happily. "I must be the luckiest person alive."

"After me," he said in a voice gruff with feeling. "What do you say we get out of here?" He slid off the table to retrieve her clothes.

Fran hopped down.

"Thank you," she said when she was dressed.

"For what?"

"Coming home."

"Home," he said. "I like the sound of that. Let's go."

"Wait. I don't want to keep our joy to myself, and Cinnamon will kill me if I don't tell her first. Would you mind if I called her right now?"

Mitch handed over his phone.

When Cinnamon picked up, Fran skipped the pleasantries. "I'm at the doctor's office and can only talk a minute. You'll never guess who's with me and what's happened…."

Five minutes later, after Cinnamon's heartfelt congratulations and Fran's promise to talk more later, the call ended and she returned his phone.

"Now I'm ready."

Hand in hand they headed for the reception area to make a second appointment.

Audrey eyed them curiously. "You two look much better than you did coming in."

"Fran and I are getting married," Mitch said.

Fran couldn't stop smiling. "And we're having a baby."

"Congratulations!" Audrey peered around them. "Did you hear that, everyone?"

Cheers and applause broke out in the reception area.

Fran scheduled next month's appointment, then started toward her friends.

Snagging her wrist, Mitch stopped her. "She'll fill you in later."

He pulled her outside, toward his car.

The second they climbed in, he kissed her.

When the both pulled back, he cleared his throat. "I made you something." He reached into the backseat and handed her a wooden bowl.

"You *made* this?" Fran stared at it. "It's beautiful."

"Foster taught me. It's not as good as I pictured it and not quite finished yet, but I'm going to ask him to show me how to polish it. Then I'll start something new. With time and practice I'll get better—the same as I will at being a good husband."

What more could a woman ask from the man she loved? "That's the sweetest thing I've ever heard," she said.

After another heart-pounding kiss, Fran smiled. "I'm not having cramps anymore."

"Then, what are we sitting in the parking lot for? Buckle up." Mitch started the car and headed for the exit.

"When and where do you want to get married?" he asked on the drive home.

"In the great room. You know Curt and Cammie Blanco? She's the best event planner around, and he's a top-notch photographer. They got married there last year, and it was a beautiful ceremony. I'd like to hire them." She remembered Andy and Sharon and frowned. "The great room's free until March, so maybe before then?"

"Sure. How about next week?"

Fran laughed. "Cammie's fast, but not that fast. How about right after Thanksgiving?"

"Okay, but no later than that. I wasted years staying at the Oceanside, not realizing I loved you. I don't want to wait anymore."

"I'm so happy," she said, beaming at him.

"So am I," Mitch said. "So am I."

Epilogue

Eleven months later

Fran let out a contented sigh and smiled down at Trevor, their four-month-old son. "I never thought I'd say this, but I thought tourist season never would end. I'm wiped out."

"You?" Mitch added a log to the crackling fire, then brushed his hands and stood. "I've never worked so hard in my life." Or felt so content and at peace. He sat down beside Fran and their child. "And I've never been so happy."

He planted a kiss on Trevor's forehead and then on Fran's sweet mouth. Love washed over him.

Fran smiled. "Did you hear that, Trevor? Your daddy's a happy man."

"Balance," they said at the same time.

"Okay if I invite Foster to dinner soon? I'll cook."

"That'd be fun. Are you going to take more lessons from him?"

"I thought I would." With tourist season over and his training program off to a good start, it was time. Also time to start a new book.

"I'm thinking about writing a book about the joys of having children," he said.

"Oh, I like that." Fran glanced at him. "You're not worried about writer's block?"

With all the love and passion in his life, Mitch could hardly remember the unhappy man he'd once been. He shook his head. "My creative well is full."

* * * * *

Watch for Ann Roth's next book,
ALL I WANT FOR CHRISTMAS,
coming November 2007,
only from Harlequin American Romance.

Welcome to cowboy country....

Turn the page for a sneak preview of
TEXAS BABY
by
Kathleen O'Brien
An exciting new title from Harlequin Superromance
for everyone who loves stories about the West.

Harlequin Superromance—
Where life and love weave together in emotional
and unforgettable ways.

CHAPTER ONE

CHASE TRANSFERRED his gaze to the road and identified a foreign spot on the horizon. A car. Almost half a mile away, where the straight, tree-lined drive met the public road. He could tell it was coming too fast, but judging the speed of a vehicle moving straight toward you was tricky.

It wasn't until it was about two hundred yards away that he realized the driver must be drunk…or crazy. Or both.

The guy was going maybe sixty. On a private drive, out here in ranch country, where kids or horses or tractors or stupid chickens might come darting out any minute, that was criminal. Chase straightened from his comfortable slouch and waved his hands.

"Slow down, you fool," he called out. He took the porch steps quickly and began walking fast down the driveway.

The car veered oddly, from one lane to another, then up onto the slight rise of the thick green spring grass. It just barely missed the fence.

"Slow down, damn it!"

He couldn't see the driver and he didn't recognize this automobile. It was small and old and couldn't have cost much, even when it was new. It was probably white, but now it needed either a wash or a new paint job or both.

"Damn it, what's wrong with you?"

At the last minute, he had to jump away, because the idiot behind the wheel clearly wasn't going to turn to avoid a collision. He couldn't believe it. The car kept coming, finally slowing a little, but it was too late.

Still going about thirty miles an hour, it slammed into the large, white-brick pillar that marked the front boundaries of the house. The pillar wasn't going to give an inch, so the car had to. The front end folded up like a paper fan.

It seemed to take forever for the car to settle, as if the trauma happened in slow motion, reverberating from the front to the back of the car in ripples of destruction. The front windshield suddenly seemed to ice over with lethal bits of glassy frost. Then the side windows exploded.

The front driver's door wrenched open, as if the car wanted to expel its contents. Metal buckled hideously. Small pieces, like hubcaps and mirrors, skipped and ricocheted insanely across the oyster-shell driveway.

Finally, everything was still. Into the silence, a plume of steam shot up like a geyser, smelling of rust and heat. Its snakelike hiss almost smothered the low, agonized moan of the driver.

Chase's anger had disappeared. He didn't feel anything but a dull sense of disbelief. Things like this didn't happen in real life. Not in his life. Maybe the sun had actually put him to sleep….

But he was already kneeling beside the car. The driver was a woman. The frosty glass-ice of the windshield was dotted with small flecks of blood. She must have hit it with her head, because just below her hair-

line a red liquid was seeping out. He touched it. He tried
to wipe it away before it reached her eyebrow, though,
of course that made no sense at all. Her eyes were shut.

Was she conscious? Did he dare move her? Her dress
was covered in glass and the metal of the car was
sticking out lethally in all the wrong places.

Then he remembered, with an intense relief, that
every good medical man in the county was here, just
behind the house, drinking his champagne. He found his
phone and paged Trent.

The woman moaned again.

Alive, then. Thank God for that.

He saw Trent coming toward him, starting out at a
lope, but quickly switching to a full run.

"Get Dr. Marchant," Chase called. "Don't bother
with 9-1-1."

Trent didn't take long to assess the situation. A fraction of a second, and he began pulling out his cell phone
and running toward the house.

The yelling seemed to have roused the woman. She
opened her eyes. They were blue and clouded with pain
and confusion.

"Chase," she said.

His breath stalled. His head pulled back. "What?"

Her only answer was another moan, and he wondered if he had imagined the word. He reached around
her and put his arm behind her shoulders. She was tiny.
Probably petite by nature, but surely way too thin. He
could feel her shoulder blades pushing against her skin,
as fragile as the wishbone in a turkey.

She seemed to have passed out, so he put his other
arm under her knees and lifted her out. He tried to avoid

the jagged metal, but her skirt caught on a piece and the tearing sound seemed to wake her again.

"No," she said. "Please."

"I'm just trying to help," he said. "It's going to be all right."

She seemed profoundly distressed. She wriggled in his arms, and she was so weak, like a broken bird. It made him feel too big and brutish. And intrusive. As if touching her this way, his bare hands against the warm skin behind her knees, was somehow a transgression.

He wished he could be more delicate. But he smelled gasoline, and he knew it wasn't safe to leave her here.

Finally he heard the sound of voices, as guests began to run around the side of the house, alerted by Trent. Dr. Marchant was at the front, racing toward them as if he were forty instead of seventy. Susannah was right behind him, her green dress floating around her trim legs.

"Please," the woman in his arms murmured again. She looked at him, the expression in her blue eyes lost and bewildered. He wondered if she might be on drugs. Hitting her head on the windshield might account for this unfocused, glazed look, but it couldn't explain the crazy driving.

"Please, put me down. Susannah… The wedding…"

Chase's arms tightened instinctively and he froze in his tracks. She whimpered, and he realized he might be hurting her. "Say that again?"

"The wedding. I have to stop it."

* * * * *

Be sure to look for TEXAS BABY,
available September 11, 2007,
as well as other fantastic Superromance titles
available in September.

Welcome to Cowboy Country...

TEXAS BABY

by Kathleen O'Brien

#1441

Chase Clayton doesn't know what to think.
A beautiful stranger has just crashed his
engagement party, demanding that he not
marry because she's pregnant with his baby.
But the kicker is—he's never seen her before.

Look for TEXAS BABY and other fantastic
Superromance titles on sale September 2007.

Available wherever books are sold.

HARLEQUIN
Super Romance

**Where life and love weave together
in emotional and unforgettable ways.**

ATHENA FORCE

Heart-pounding romance and thrilling adventure.

Professional negotiator Lindsey Novak is faced with her biggest challenge—to buy back Teal Arnett, a young woman with unique powers. In the process Lindsey uncovers a devastating plot that involves scientists from around the globe, and all of them lead to one woman who is bent on destroying Athena Academy...at any cost.

LOOK FOR

THE GOOD THIEF

by Judith Leon

Available September wherever you buy books.

REQUEST YOUR FREE BOOKS.
2 FREE NOVELS PLUS 2
FREE GIFTS!

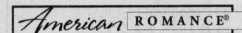

American **ROMANCE®**

Heart, Home & Happiness!

YES! Please send me 2 FREE Harlequin American Romance® novels and my 2
FREE gifts. After receiving them, if I don't wish to receive any more books, I can return
the shipping statement marked "cancel." If I don't cancel, I will receive 4 brand-new
novels every month and be billed just $4.24 per book in the U.S., or $4.99 per book in
Canada, plus 25¢ shipping and handling per book and applicable taxes, if any*. That's
a savings of close to 15% off the cover price! I understand that accepting the 2 free
books and gifts places me under no obligation to buy anything. I can always return a
shipment and cancel at any time. Even if I never buy another book from Harlequin, the
two free books and gifts are mine to keep forever.   154 HDN EEZK 354 HDN EEZV

Name	(PLEASE PRINT)
Address	Apt. #
City	State/Prov.	Zip/Postal Code

Signature (if under 18, a parent or guardian must sign)

Mail to the **Harlequin Reader Service®**:
IN U.S.A.: P.O. Box 1867, Buffalo, NY 14240-1867
IN CANADA: P.O. Box 609, Fort Erie, Ontario L2A 5X3

Not valid to current Harlequin American Romance subscribers.

Want to try two free books from another line?
Call 1-800-873-8635 or visit www.morefreebooks.com.

* Terms and prices subject to change without notice. NY residents add applicable sales tax.
Canadian residents will be charged applicable provincial taxes and GST. This offer is limited to
one order per household. All orders subject to approval. Credit or debit balances in a customer's
account(s) may be offset by any other outstanding balance owed by or to the customer. Please
allow 4 to 6 weeks for delivery.

Your Privacy: Harlequin is committed to protecting your privacy. Our Privacy
Policy is available online at www.eHarlequin.com or upon request from the Reader
Service. From time to time we make our lists of customers available to reputable
firms who may have a product or service of interest to you. If you would
prefer we not share your name and address, please check here. ☐

HAR

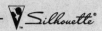

SPECIAL EDITION™

Look for

BACHELOR NO MORE

by Victoria Pade

Jared Perry finds more than he's looking for when he and Mara Pratt work together to clear Celeste Perry's name. Celeste is Jared's grandmother and is being investigated as an accomplice to a robbery, after she abandoned her husband and two sons. But are they prepared for what they discover?

Northbridge Nuptials

Available September wherever you buy books.

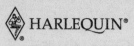

HARLEQUIN®

American ROMANCE®

COMING NEXT MONTH

#1177 TWIN SURPRISE by Jacqueline Diamond
Times Two
Marta Lawson is secretly in love with police officer and playboy Derek Reed.
When her friends put in a bid at a bachelor auction, her birthday present turns
out to be a few glorious hours with the town lady-killer! It's a fantasy come
true—except about a month later she finds her "dream" date has resulted in not
one surprise, but two....

#1178 DANCING WITH DALTON by Laura Marie Altom
Fatherhood
Dance instructor Rose Vasquez was widowed two years ago, and even though her
six-year-old daughter lights up her life, her world is not complete. Buying a dance
studio allows Rose to throw herself into teaching, but she never expected to find
amongst her new students a man who makes her feel so gloriously alive....

#1179 HOME FOR A HERO by Mary Anne Wilson
Shelter Island Stories
Lucas Roman had retreated to Shelter Island to heal wounds he'd suffered in
his tour of duty. Physically, he was fine, but the reason he'd chosen exile was a
closely guarded secret. Lucas thought he had his new life worked out, but then
his prized solitude was shattered by Shay Donovan, a woman who, literally,
invaded his private beach....

#1180 ONE STUBBORN TEXAN by Kara Lennox
Russ Klein has a perfect small-town life—until a big-city detective named
Sydney Baines discovers he's a long-lost heir with a big inheritance. Preserving
his family means refusing the money, which also means asking the dainty sleuth
to forget he exists. But Sydney has her own reasons for needing Russ to take the
money—and she's not backing down!

www.eHarlequin.com

HARCNM0807